LEGACY ACADEMY

LEGACY ACADEMY

A. P. Goodman

ISBN 979-8-9872709-0-5 (large print paperback)

Book Cover by Nitish Mathpal

Visit us on the Web!
www.apgoodman.com

First edition 2023

To my Bug.

May you always trailblaze your own
path and never lose your fighting
spirit.

I love you unconditionally.

Table of Contents

Chapter 1
Cardboard and Car Rides

The room smelled like cardboard. Though, to be fair, the whole house did. Cardboard and dust. Towers of boxes were stacked every couple of feet. It looked more like Lena was moving out than moving in. This was her new home now. At least it was new in terms of occupancy. Lena wanted to be surprised that this house was so run-down but, with her parents, life tended to be easier when she expected the unexpected. Despite their best intentions, their actions always came across as a bit absurd. She flopped on the bed with a sigh. A cloud of dust puffed in her face.

"Disgusting," Lena said with a scowl.

"Magdalena, is that you?" her mom called from down the hall.

"Yeah Mom, I just found some dust bunnies." She gestured to the entire room behind her closed door.

"Isn't it great? It gives this place such charm!" Lena could hear her mom's footsteps patter down the stairs.

Charm. That was not an adjective Lena would have used. Charm was what freshly cleaned houses with open rooms and endless possibilities had. Charm smelled like brand-new construction. Not that Lena had ever experienced that before, but she felt pretty confident about her conjecture. Glancing around, she noticed cobwebs hanging from the end of her curtain rods. She hung her head in disappointment.

Turning to daydreams, Lena imagined some people would pay good money for an old house, especially with some history behind it. Images of cobwebs, creaky floorboards, and damp cellars coated in moss created an eerie scene in her mind. She could even see how a house like that could have charm. Regardless, that was not her current situation here either. Lena estimated this place was probably built in the early 2000s. It was just—

"Abandoned." The word was eager to escape her lips.

Her parents had seemingly jumped at the chance to move, and despite a full day traveling in the car, Lena still could not come up with a single reason why. Their previous house wasn't a cherished heirloom by any means, but it was the house Lena grew up in. School wasn't great back where she came from, but it was fine. In fact, she used that word a lot to describe her life. Everything was pretty much fine all the time. Her house. Her school. Her friends. Her family. Herself. It was all fine. That answer was basically a reflex at this point.

There was a knock at the door. "Hey. How are you doing, honey? Everything going alright here?"

"Yup! Everything's fine!" Lena amused herself as her dad stepped into her room.

"I know it seems like a lot of work now, but it'll be worth it. This place will be feeling like home in no time!"

"I'm sure of it. Can't wait, Dad." Lena forced a smile. He winced. He always knew when she was faking. Darn parents.

"Things really will get better, Magpie. I promise." He walked into the room and gave her a hug.

"It's okay, really." She lightly squeezed him back. Even through the heavy stench of the room, the aroma of her dad's woodworking prevailed. When Lena was little, it used to be a fun game to guess which wood he had worked with earlier in the day. She'd snuggle up close to him at bedtime to form her best guesses. She gave into the hug more than she'd originally intended to. "I just didn't think anything was bad to begin with."

"It wasn't bad where we were. You're right, but it'll be better here." He loosened his grip. "That said, I have to admit I'm disappointed. I thought, for sure, you were going to guess cedar." He pulled back with a smirk and a wink.

Lena rolled her eyes in jest. "I wouldn't hold your breath for that one, Dad."

"Ah, why's that?" he asked as he headed towards the door.

"Because we're both keenly aware you smell like smoked hickory," Lena asserted, giving him a stern look.

His smile brimmed from ear to ear. As she closed the door, she could hear him yell, "That's my girl!"

She looked around the room. Her room. Even the thought of that made her uncomfortable. Nothing in there felt like it was hers—except, potentially, for all the moving boxes. Those probably belonged to her as long as her mom didn't do the organizing. Not only had her parents moved at the drop of a dime, but they had moved into a fully-furnished house. A fully-furnished, abandoned house. Lena was struggling to get over it.

"I am not unpacking in this sty," she said defiantly to the filth before her. "I need a plan. I guess step one needs to be finding cleaning supplies. Step two will be to unpack." She picked up the musty comforter on her bed and immediately threw it into the far corner of the room, watching as the dust cascaded down its folds. Lena hunched over, gagging. She piled all the fabric she could on top of the comforter's mound, opened her door, and started kicking it toward the stairs. "Incoming!"

~~~~~~~~~~~~~~~~~~~~~~~~~~~~~~~~~~~~

The sun gleamed into Lena's curtainless room. She breathed in the fragrance of lemony disinfectant. Her initial idea to start a bonfire using all of the house's contents was swiftly shut down, but she had been able to convince her parents to toss all the linens. Lena wanted to find what she could in the moving boxes that day and then go shopping later that week. While she was visualizing what she wanted her new space to look like, she almost forgot she had awoken to the sound of a doorbell.

"Magdalena! You have a friend here! How exciting!"

Lena could hear people making their way up the stairs. "Mom, what are you—" Lena's doorknob started to turn. "No!" She leaped out of bed to close the door.

"He's a boy!" her mom whispered loudly from the other side. "Don't tell Dad!"

"I'm not—" She sighed. "I need five minutes!" *Stay calm*, she told herself as she rushed to get ready. There was no use in arguing. Her mom's attention span didn't last long enough for arguments. With no time and no room for escape, brushing her teeth was out of the question. Gum was going to have to do for now. "I am not a praying person, Lord, but please let me live through this," she begged before entering the hall.

He was tall and lanky. Probably around her age, she guessed. Also, as she feared, they'd likely go to school together. Luckily, he didn't give the appearance of being super popular, and at this point, that was a huge relief.

He waved, trying to interrupt Lena's thoughts. "Hey?"

"Hey...." She looked around for her mom. Nothing. Her mom had left him all alone waiting for Lena outside her door. "I'm so sorry."

He laughed reassuringly. "No, it's okay. I have parents too."

"I'm Lena." She offered a handshake.

"Hey, Lena. I'm Tao." He bowed then noticed her hand. He reached out, but it was too late. An awkward silence set in.

Lena tried to initiate small talk. "So, do you come here often?"

"To the upper floor of your house? Not so much. I try to avoid entering the residences of strangers." He could see Lena's face start to blanch. "But we're friends now, so it's all good. Right? I mean I'm pretty sure that's what I heard your mom say." He chuckled.

"Yeah. Hey, actually, about that, why are you here?"

Tao's eyes widened at her question. He went to speak, but nothing came out.

"Wait! No! I mean ... like ... argh." Lena stopped for a second to regain her composure. "What I meant was, what brings you around..." *My mom. My house.* "... my bedroom?" *Nope, that was wrong.* "Other than my mother?" *That was worse.* Lena cringed; she wanted to disappear.

"How about we go outside? I could use some fresh air. Plus, your mom hired me to give you a tour of the town and show you where our main store is."

"Leaving here sounds fabulous." That was the best idea she'd heard all day.

"Great, grab your things and I'll be in the yellow car outside."

"Aww, yellow like a taxicab!" Lena joked. He didn't laugh. Her heart started to race again. She did NOT want to be going around her new town, and seeing other people from her school, in a taxi.

"Don't stress out. Just meet me outside." Tao vanished down the stairs.

Lena hurried to brush her teeth, freshen up, and grab her purse from her room. She could see the road from her uncovered windows. To look or not to look, that was the question at hand. *Please don't be a taxi, please don't be a taxi, please don't be a taxi.* Lena attempted to will her wish into existence, but it was no use. Only one type of vehicle came in that kind of mustard yellow.

~~~~~~~~~~~~~~~~~~~~~~~~~~~~~~~

"Welcome to Astoria." Tao pointed to a nearby sign. "We have pretty much one of everything when it comes to buildings and a whole bunch of things when it comes to nature. Our town hall and police station combo are on the right, and the fire station is up there on the left. We have exactly one school, although that is sort of a cheat being that it's technically two buildings." He yammered on. He had clearly done this too many times.

"There's only one school? For everyone?" Lena asked, surprised.

"You got it. Kindergarten through twelfth grade. We're kind of all-inclusive here in Astoria."

"Wow. There must not be a lot of people here then, huh?" As she peered into the distant parking lots, she noticed a severe lack of other cars.

"There's enough, but you're correct. Astoria's population is less than average, especially considering how large the town is. Our whereabouts are really unique because three sides of the city are surrounded by water and the fourth side is all mountains. There are roads in and out; no one is trapped here by any means, but we certainly face a good amount of natural isolation. Even businesses tend not to have a lot of interest in coming to Astoria. My parents love to tell stories of how hard they had it before supercenters existed."

"I can't imagine living like that," remarked Lena.

"Me neither, actually. As long as I can remember, Astoria's had everything I've ever needed. I've never felt the urge to travel anywhere else," Tao said, glancing over to see Lena's reaction. Astoria tended to bring in an eclectic assortment of people. You had to be a little different to want to live there. As anticipated, Lena looked shocked. Out-of-towners were so predictable.

"Here's my stop." Lena started to gather her things. "Are you sure you're okay waiting?"

"Yeah, you won't need a hand carrying anything?" He pulled into a parking space up front.

"As long as you have shopping carts here, I'll be just fine," she teased.

"How original. I guarantee I've never heard that one before." The sarcasm was heavy in his voice. "Enjoy your time. I'll be right here. No rush." As Lena left, he reclined his seat and put his hat over his eyes.

The store was bigger than she'd imagined. On the outside, it had seemed like any other supercenter. On the inside, it was immense. A delicious pumpkin-apple haze welcomed customers as they entered. Lena had a hard time seeing where the aisles ended. Thankfully, there were signs everywhere. She grabbed a cart and, after nabbing one of the featured candles, headed off to the home and garden section. Some things were too hard to resist.

About twenty minutes had passed when she knocked on Tao's passenger window. Slightly confused, he rolled the window down. "Everything okay, Lena?"

"Yup, all done. Can you unlock the car so I can unload my bags?"

Tao chuckled. "No locked doors here; help yourself." He started to put her bags in.

"Why? What if someone tries to break in?"

"I'm sure if someone did, then people would start to lock up, but that isn't really commonplace here." He finished putting the bags away and opened her door. "After you, madame."

Lena was quiet most of the ride home. Astoria made her feel uneasy. Either Tao was far too naive about his hometown, which was almost guaranteed, or this place was just off. He had talked about the town being isolated earlier, but the vibe of Astoria felt more like a living time capsule. She watched as the houses passed by. There weren't a lot of cookie-cutter neighborhoods around. Each dwelling was a little bit different than the next, yet they all were immaculate. She watched one pristine abode pass after the next until that façade came to a grinding halt.

"What is that place?" Lena asked, repulsed. To say the yard was overgrown was an understatement. There were thick, dark green leaves everywhere. She had originally thought they descended from a nearby tree in the yard, but the vines were spread out in every direction. "It's a mess!"

Tao pulled over. "That is the Old Hag's place."

"The Old Hag? Who's that?" Lena couldn't stop staring. "And what've they got hidden in there?" She hurried out of the car to take a closer look.

"Lena! Hey! I don't know, but come back. Let's go home, okay?" Tao followed over to where she was pointing. The object was small and white. Whatever it was, it was buried deep within the foliage. He quickly withdrew his stare. "Come on." He reached for her hand.

Lena slinked away. "What is this place?" The yard carried all the humidity of a greenhouse, despite being outside. Its scent was similar too. The odors of soil, leaves, bugs, and pollen were overwhelming. Lena was unable to spot any flowers yet still knew they existed somewhere in that condensed ecosystem. "I want to go in."

"No. Absolutely not. That is completely out of the question. It's time to go home, Lena. My tour is over. Let's get your bags and call it a day." Tao was opening the trunk when it slammed shut. Lena jumped, startled. She could hear Tao yelling at someone. She spun, glancing back.

Two people on skateboards were kicking the taxi. Lena assumed they were also boys around her age, but with their Halloween masks on, it was hard to tell. They were loud and pushing Tao like a ball from one bully to the other.

"Hey! Knock that off!" Lena stormed over to the car. She pushed one of them. He didn't move an inch. She was reminded at this moment that she had more emotions than she did physical strength. Her impulse was quickly turning into regret.

"Oh, look what we have here! A newbie! And Tao's already hired her as his bodyguard. How cute." He snatched her arm forcefully. His friend left Tao and started to snigger as he walked over to a dangling Lena.

"Enough! Leave her be." Anger was rising in Tao's voice.

She wondered if she was actually in danger. The bully let go of her arm. Lena looked for an out, but they had blocked her in. She couldn't tell the differences between them, even up close. Were they twins? Regardless, they were certainly huge, muscular, and brutish. The one on the right pushed her and she fell into a sitting position on top of the car's hood. She winced as it burned her thighs. The boys both smiled simultaneously at her pain.

"Some bodyguard you are," the bully barked in her face, pretending, she hoped, to bite. The one on the left followed in sync. Their aggression was too much. She needed an out. Lena swung her legs over the other side of the car, kicking past one of the bullies, and ran as fast as she could—straight into the Old Hag's house.

It took Lena a moment to realize where she was at first. Her only goal had been to escape. It wasn't until she locked a door behind her and sank to the floor that she processed her actions. Rustling noises came from the floor above her. Of course, it only made sense that she wouldn't be the only one here. Lena had just broken into the Old Hag's house! She stood up and tried to straighten herself out.

"Hello? My name's Lena; I'm new here." As if that was a sufficient reason for entering a house without permission. There was no response. She peeked out the window. There was a wall of hunter-green leaves obstructing her view. Lena tried to spot any sight of mustard yellow through the scarce openings, but there was none to be found. Tao was gone.

"Fantastic. I've committed a crime and the only person who could tell me how to get home is gone. Awesome first day, Lena. You're crushing it." She ridiculed herself as she kept peering out the window. Maybe if Tao had left, the bullies would have gone too.

Near the base of the window, a bright white sign stood out against the dark background. "Open house. Showings from 12:00 p.m. – 3:00 p.m."

Lena looked down at her watch; it was 2:00 p.m. "Fu—"

"Ah! Stop right there, please!" a strong female voice commanded. There was a long pause afterwards. Lena felt paralyzed. "Turn around, if you'd be so kind." The lady tapped Lena's shoulder.

"I'm so sorry! I—" The Old Hag held up a hand to stop her. Not only was she surprisingly elderly, but she held a remarkable staff. Not even Lena's dad could create something that intricate.

"I saw the whole thing. Those boys can be quite a handful, but that's no excuse to break into someone else's home. Is it?" The lady's eyes narrowed on Lena.

"Yes, ma'am.... Oh, I mean no, ma'am." Lena was stammering.

The Old Hag nodded. "All right then. Let's get you situated before my client comes home."

"Oh." There was a sense of relief. "So, you're not the Old—"

The lady pounded her staff on the ground. "Enough! You've already entered uninvited; let us not make things worse by talking about that which we don't understand. Understood?" Lena tried to shake her head. She wasn't sure if the correct answer to that question was yes or no. "Follow me," the woman instructed.

As Lena looked to follow her guide, she noticed the living space was actually very refreshing on the inside. The decor was all done in pure white and gray. There was beauty in its simplicity. The greenhouse smell, however, still permeated inside.

"Thank you," Lena said softly. The lady turned with a curious expression.

"For?"

"For getting me out of a bad situation. I've never been bullied before." Lena tugged on her clothes nervously. "It's a lot scarier in person than in the movies." Her voice was almost inaudible.

"Listen, I'm not going to say it's permissible that you barged into some stranger's house. However, those boys wouldn't have stopped of their own accord. So, it was smart to get out. You need to look out for yourself better next time. You don't want to run from one source of panic to something unknown that ends up far worse."

"Yes, ma'am."

The woman laughed kindly at Lena. They were at the back door.

"Your parents taught you well. There are only a special few in my school who call me 'ma'am.'"

"Your school?"

"Correct. Legacy Academy is the primary school in Astoria and it just so happens to currently be mine."

"Oh." This was not going to be a one-time interaction then. This was going to be a five-times-a-week interaction. Fantastic. "I start there tomorrow."

"I figured as much. I presume you are Magdalena Basil?"

Lena nodded, defeated. "Yes, ma'am."

"Nice to meet you, Miss Basil. I'm Principal Chromwell."

Chapter 2

Lockers and Lectures

"Okay Magpie, we're here. Ready for your first day of school?" Her dad parked the car. Legacy Academy was massive. It mirrored a gray, cobblestone, European castle. Its paved entryway was more elegant than any she'd seen on TV. Lena seriously wondered if a valet was going to approach their vehicle. How could Tao say that there wasn't anything unique in Astoria? Lena was awestruck. She bid farewell to her dad and headed towards the school.

On the inside, Legacy was as intimidating as it was astounding. Students were everywhere. There were hundreds, at minimum, in the foyer alone. They covered the grand staircases and the benches; they were even sprawled out on the floor. It was hard to take a single step without being on top of someone or their belongings. Lena barely found her way through the common area. If there were signs, they weren't visible. When she finally discovered the halls of lockers, she was relieved. Not only had she made it to her first destination of the day, but now she had some personal space too.

"Phew. Okay. Let's see. We're in the 2100s and currently I'm at...." She looked down at her registration paper. "2918."

"Lena!" Tao called, rushing over to her.

She met him with a glare. "If it isn't the escape artist himself."

"What? No. It wasn't like that. I just—"

"You just bailed on me the first second you could. I didn't even know how to get home!"

"I bailed? You couldn't stay in the car and then you ran straight into that awful house. What was I supposed to do? And how could you not know you lived just a few houses down from there? It's not like it blends in."

"Hmm. I don't know, Tao. Maybe because I've only lived here a day? Maybe because I was terrified out of my mind when those ogres were barking in my face?!" Lena was yelling at this point.

"Okay. Okay. Shh. Trust me. Calm down." Tao pulled her to a nearby bench in a little nook. "Listen. I get it, alright? But, for both our sakes, can you not start our day by screaming about ogres in the school? You don't want to cause a scene in your first fifteen minutes here, do you?"

Lena huffed; she knew he was right. She didn't want to be labeled as some crazy girl screaming in the hallway before she could even find her locker. "Fine, but what you did made me feel horrible. You couldn't even drop my bags off after your great escape."

"They're in my trunk right now for safekeeping. I was hoping I'd bump into you at school today. I wanted to offer you a ride home and carry your bags in. You don't even have to pay me for yesterday."

"Excuse me?! Pay you?! Why on earth would I pay you?" Her voice was escalating again.

Perplexed, Tao explained, "When your mom called to order the tour, she said she would pay me at the end because she didn't know how long it would take. I thought it'd be considerate to waive that, given what happened."

"Oh." Lena had completely forgotten he was hired to help. She had almost considered him a friend. "My mistake. Thank you. Next time we're in need of your service, we'll be sure to pay you, if and when you actually get me home safely." Now she was just being rude.

"Whatever. Do you need help finding anything or should I meet you at your locker after school?" Tao was getting irritated with how much work this new girl was.

Lena shrank a little. He had been her only chance at a friend so far and she was blowing it. Her enrollment papers were getting mangled by her nervous fidgeting.

"I'm sorry if I offended you. I forgot we weren't actually friends." She felt so embarrassed. That did not sound any better aloud than it did in her head.

"I'm sure it's overwhelming walking into this school without any familiarity. Legacy can be quite the maze when you haven't grown up here. Come on, I'll take you to your locker." Tao reached for her registration. "2918. You're not too far from it. Let's go this way." He pushed ahead. "And hey, I'm sorry about the Beboy twins. They're a lot for anyone to handle."

Lena had a million questions as she followed him. Mostly, they revolved around those horrible brutish twins. For instance, how likely were they to be "a lot for anyone to handle" in her near future? Also, did that mean people could actually handle them? If so, where could she find such people? These were all queries Lena wanted immediate answers to.

~~~~~~~~~~~~~~~~~~~~~~~~~~~~

There was a letter-sized sticky note attached to Lena's locker when she and Tao arrived.

"Good morning, Miss Basil. I trust this finds you well. After you have deposited your items in your assigned receptacle, please head to the Chambers of the Headmistress. You will likely find me there, though if I am not in my allocated space at this time, I beseech you to wait. Good day to you and I will see you soon!

P.S. Should you not be able to navigate Legacy Academy by its posted signage, and should another student be unable to assist you, simply lift this correspondence and it will become a map for you and you alone. Once more, I bid you adieu and count upon your prompt arrival."

"Is it just me or is Principal Chromwell ridiculously hard to understand? I never know how I'm supposed to respond." Lena tried to peel the sticky note off to the side, but it didn't budge.

"You get a feel for her after a while. She's just from a different generation." Tao read the message over Lena's shoulder. "Lift up."

"What?"

"The note. Lift up." He motioned to her.

She eyed him irritably then did as he suggested. It came off as easy as a sticky note should. "What's the joke?" She opened her locker and unloaded her backpack.

"The joke?" Tao didn't understand.

"Yeah, with the sticky. No matter how much strength I used, it didn't tear off. Is it like some newbie prank? Or like a light hazing, where everyone gets to walk by and laugh?" Lena paused for insight, but Tao didn't respond. "That's kind of lame coming from the headmistress, don't you think? I didn't expect an eighty-year-old to be playing practical jokes." Lena's rude tone resurfaced. Tao noticed she used this tone a lot.

"No one's out here to get you, Lena. However, if you want my two cents—" she responded by dramatically shaking her head no "—which clearly you don't, I'd try to drop the attitude before you go to meet Principal Chromwell. She tends to get along with everyone, but being disrespectful the second you get here isn't going to go over well. Try to be more open-minded and a little less judgmental." Tao picked up Lena's backpack from the floor.

"I'm not judgmental. It's not my fault that everything's so weird in Astoria, or Legacy, or whatever!" She slammed her locker shut.

Tao raised his eyebrows. "Do you hear what you sound like? Or...."

"Yes. I hear it too." She took her backpack and sighed. "Can we go, please?"

"This way." Tao turned into a nearby corridor.

This hall was smaller than the hallways off the common areas. Oversized decorations filled the walls. They smelled musty. Chunky gold frames, filled with paintings of people she didn't recognize, went on endlessly. The walls behind the frames were crimson with a white woven design. Embellished gold crowns were centered into their woven loops. She ran her fingers along the top of the half-wall paneling. Tao was explaining something. He could ramble on about anything. Thankfully, Lena was exceptionally proficient at ignoring long, drawn-out speeches.

The art around her depicted dragons, wizards, and royalty. She paused, touching a picture of a queen bestowing a necklace of flowers onto a knight.

"Lena? You've stopped walking."

"Sorry, this picture caught me. It reminded me of something from when I was a kid. We can keep going."

"You know that picture?" Tao's eyes lit up in excitement.

"Well, I mean not that picture exactly." She was feeling uncomfortable again. "When I was little, I loved visiting this place I called 'The Castle.' It was a replica, of course, kind of like this school. There were tons of shops as soon as you walked inside. Trinkets twinkled all around the big gathering room. It was so pretty. Then you'd be escorted to your seat, where you'd have dinner and wait for the show to start. When the servers would come, they even pretended the food was from magical beasts; it was so silly. During dinner, the knights would joust and whoever won would get flowers from the queen to throw into the crowd. I loved that part, I always wanted the flowers. I mean who doesn't want a hot guy tossing them a rose, right?" Lena was lost in happy memories and excitement.

"Me." Tao's eyes had glossed over.

Lena scoffed. "You're the one who asked."

"I know. I regret doing so."

She feigned offense. "We can keep going; I didn't know stopping required a full investigation."

"I'm slightly distracted by how you phrased your complaint, but it's better than listening to some corporation playing pretend, so we are in agreement." A bell rang. Tao looked at his watch. "I have to go. Even if I got a pass, it's not worth listening to my professor turning it into today's lesson. Keep going straight until you see the drying herbs and her door is past the cauldron on the right."

"What? Did you say cauldron? And why would your professor obsess over a hall pass? Is he one of those teachers that are crazy about being on time? I had one of those back home in Arizona. They're the worst." Lena sympathized.

"Sort of. My first class is Sacred Writings and Symbols. He gets excited over anything written. At any rate, you'll be fine! Don't forget to turn right at the cauldron." He opened a door that led to another hallway and disappeared into it.

Lena was so confused. Why was there a door to a hallway? More so, who had cauldrons in their school? She remembered a display at the supercenter.

"Oh, right. It's Halloween," she said, reassuring herself.

It wasn't long before the walls turned from crimson and gold to a muted purple. Long dark strands of varying lengths hung from above. Attached were bundles of prickly plants. The light was slowly starting to fade as Lena went further into the passageway.

"Ouch!" A low-hanging weed poked through her clothes. Lena noticed a faint orange glow up ahead. Despite treading carefully, another sprig jabbed her arm. She checked to see if it was bleeding. "These better not be poisonous. I'm not getting some type of skin reaction on my first day here."

"They're not poisonous, Magdalena, but to assess the likelihood of an allergic reaction, I would need your medical history. I'm sure your father has had his hands extremely full, but I'm confident he will send it along soon enough." There stood Principal Chromwell, brightly illuminated in orange light, stirring a humongous working cauldron.

~~~~~~~~~~~~~~~~~~~~~~~~~~~~~~

"You may sit here." A large stained-glass window filtered the room's only source of light. It cast a deep shadow of the headmistress' silhouette into her chamber. The power Principal Chromwell wielded was not subtle. Lena had been directed to a high-backed velvet chair, similar to a throne. "I rarely get visitors here in my chambers. Welcome. I didn't expect you to come through the back entrance; most students are unaware of that corridor's existence. In fact, all are ignorant except one. I assume that means Mr. Vovi gave you an ample tour of the abundant archives we have displayed there?"

"Yes ma'am. I think so?" *Was Mr. Vovi Tao?*

The headmistress chortled. "He is always able to provide a historical explanation, no matter what the environment, is he not?" Lena's face showed no reaction. "Irregardless, let me formally welcome you, Miss Basil, to Legacy Academy. Legacy Academy is one of the only schools of its kind. It has a rich history dating back hundreds of thousands of years." Lena thought to interject, but Principal Chromwell appeared wistful. "You'll find almost anything you want within the academy and possibly even more. Our classes cover everything from rudimentary education to the most advanced sciences of our time. Your customized class schedule is founded on what I've assessed your basic levels to be. It would be impractical to assume that you'll fancy every teacher you encounter, but I assure you that they will always promote you when you are ready. This will remain true regardless of what that time frame may be."

Lena raised her hand and started to speak. "Wouldn't my class level increase at the end of the school year?"

"No, Miss Basil. Legacy is an academy based on individualized skill sets. As a student progresses, so will their courses. Unfortunately, the opposite is also true. Should a student choose to not apply themselves in their studies, their level will be held indefinitely."

"Indefinitely? Doesn't high school only last four years?"

"Outside of classes, Legacy Academy offers a vast array of extracurricular activities. They are available in abundance and we are always eager for new members. I imagine you'll find what you're looking for straight away. Are there any activities you'd like to join forthwith?"

"No thanks." Lena enjoyed physical activity but preferred being on her own.

"Very well, then. I shall give you your schedule and walk you to your first class after one final mention. I'd like you to understand the rules here. They are very important. We only have a few, but it's absolutely essential that you follow them explicitly. Do you understand, Miss Basil?"

Lena nodded.

"All right, then. Legacy Academy has five main sections all connected by our palatial courtyard at their center—the elementary area, the upperclassmen area, the shared common area, the open outdoor area, and the student housing dorms. The academy obviously has a small administrative portion as well, but it's not prominent to our academy's structure. Now, it is imperative that you never venture out of your assigned section without permission. I try to let students move around as freely as possible, but, especially with new students, it's much safer for everyone involved to stay within their designated areas. Legacy Academy is exceedingly expansive and I think you'll find it much larger than it appears. Recently traversed hallways may take you someplace entirely new and may not always lead you back from whence you came, if you're not careful. You need to keep your wits about you and use more than simply your eyes to get around. Do you understand, Miss Basil?"

Not in the slightest. Lena wondered if she'd ever have a conversation with the principal where she understood what was going on. *It's just a school,* she thought. A very, very big school, but it was still just a school. Lena had been navigating buildings like these for most of her life. "Yup, got it! I won't go anywhere I'm not supposed to. I did have one question though." She had Principal's Chromwell's full attention. Lena found it slightly intimidating. "You said one of the five sections of the building was student housing?"

"Indeed I did."

"Am I going to have to move here?"

There was another chuckle from the headmistress. "Don't be silly, Miss Basil. I understand the challenges of your current living situation, but even that would not have slipped past your parents. No. Not all students live on our grounds. For some, it makes much more sense financially to stay home. For others, the travel would be inconceivable, so it's best they stay here. There are all sorts of reasons out there for why each family has opted for one choice or the other, but it would be impossible to apply one solution to everybody."

That was reassuring. Lena may not have understood much of what the principal said, but she was confident she didn't have to live there and that was enough. "Thank you."

Principal Chromwell smiled at her. "You'll figure it all out. I expect great things from you, Magdalena Basil. I think you'll find Legacy Academy to be a perfect fit. Now, here is your class schedule. I saw in Arizona you had incredibly impressive marks in your English and Latin classes. It inspired me to take the liberty of assigning your first lesson to be Languages of Today and Beyond. I do hope you enjoy it. Shall we go?"

Why does every class here have such a strange name? She had only heard of two, but where was good old History or Literature?

She'd even settle for Language Arts.

"If you have a map, I'd be happy to navigate myself," Lena offered. The headmistress eyed her suspiciously. "I won't go anywhere uninvited. I promise."

"I suppose that would be fine. Follow the signs. Be steadfast. If you get lost, use the message from your locker. The map there will help you."

"Okay ma'am. I appreciate it." Lena gathered up her things.

"Good luck, Miss Basil. I wish you all the best. May we not meet again until the time is right." Principal Chromwell stood up from behind her ornamented desk.

Lena nodded as she rose from the heavy velvet chair, bowed politely, and rushed out the room's main door.

~~~~~~~~~~~~~~~~~~~~~~~~~~~~~~

The air was instantly lighter in the hallway. *Why do I always freak out in front of the principal? Did I just bow? Who does that?* In her fourteen plus years of existence, she had never bowed to anyone, until today. She wanted to hit her head against the nearest wall.

A bell rang. She pulled out her schedule: Languages of Today and Beyond in room 1007. She recognized she was in one of the common areas from earlier that morning. The hallways filled instantaneously. It was hard for

Lena to orient herself with the little knowledge she had. She was starting to get pushed around by the crowd and dropped her schedule. Panic set in; she needed that paper to get around, but it was too risky to pick it up. Lena was struggling to keep her footing as it was.

"Move, move, move!" A figure came right at her, pushing Lena towards a wall. Her heart was racing. Her footing slipped and she began to fall. The figure caught her. "Five more steps backwards, keep going." Lena did as she was told and ended up falling into a desk tucked into an alcove. The crowd bustled behind the tall muscular figure in front of Lena.

"I dropped my class list and my map. I need to go back," Lena pleaded with lackluster effort. She could see the crowd was thinning out.

"Don't worry; I got it for you. I saw it fall and wasn't sure who it belonged to at first. Turns out you were easy to spot; you looked like a cub stuck in a stampede. You alright?" They offered her the piece of mangled paper. It had footprints all over it.

My pride isn't, Lena thought. "Yeah, thanks. I'm new, if that isn't apparent."

"It is rather obvious." They attempted to tame a strand of their rainbow-colored hair. Lena watched as it sprung right back up.

"I was afraid of that. I'm Lena." A second ring of the bell sounded. "And now I've made you late. I'm sorry." She stood up.

"Nah, don't worry about it. I'm good at talking my way out of things. Most people call me Simon. Want some help getting to your first class? I can also give you a heads-up on any teachers if I know them. Some professors have been here forever."

"That'd be great." Lena showed Simon her schedule.

They scoffed. "That's the easiest roster I've ever seen!"

"Oh...." Sheepishly, Lena tucked it away.

"Don't be like that. I only meant that you have the best teachers around. They're all really approachable and friendly." Simon waited for Lena to relax more. "Pop quiz! If you were going to go to room 1007, which way would you head?"

There were doors to a garden straight ahead and huge barren hallways on the sides. "I don't know. I thought I could head straight, I remember Principal Chromwell saying something about a star layout, but this doesn't look familiar anymore."

"I could tell you got lost in the shuffle. I wouldn't focus too much on logistics around here. I'll give you some tips to help, but when in doubt just avoid the mob until you can control your own pace. You don't want to be carried into somewhere unexpectedly."

Who cares if I end up in the gym instead of science class? How bad could that possibly be?

Simon guided Lena out the doors to the courtyard. They shared advice on navigating Legacy Academy while showing her the right path to take. They promptly arrived in front of Lena's class.

"All you from here on out. Good luck. Oh, and Mr. Babel is a talker. If you can hold a good conversation, he won't give you a problem."

"Babel? Like the tower?" Lena asked curiously.

"Anyways, I gotta go. Take care, little cub!" With a brief wink Simon was off and Lena was alone once again.

Chapter 3

Friends and Frustrations

Entering her first class was about as awful as Lena expected it to be. When she walked in, she was suddenly aware of an instant silence passing over the crowd and thirty people staring directly at her. She froze. She stared back and silently waved her admission papers in the air like a white flag.

"Ah, gratissimum, Miss Basil!" Mr. Babel, recognizing a soul in need, transitioned smoothly.

"Hi," Lena said, forcing a half smile.

"Non loqueris Latine?" he inquired quizzically.

She shook her head no. "Non, solum Anglicus."

"A jokester! I like it! Have a seat back there! We just started!" Mr. Babel seemed very excitable.

Lena walked to the back of the class and took an empty seat. She was happy to have a place to sit for a while. She reached into her bag for her materials. There were no textbooks. Dismayed, she took out a notebook instead. *That probably would've been a good question for the principal*, Lena thought. Pushing off her concerns, she focused back on Mr. Babel. He spoke fast and moved around a lot. He had a lot of energy.

A majority of the students in front of her were zoned out or goofing off. Lena felt relieved to be back in a familiar environment. Written on the board was, "Today's Lesson: Latin." Class seemed pretty self-explanatory.

Lena heard some snickering beside her. "Hey newbie! Legacy or Descendant?" They flicked a paper ball her way. She tried to ignore it but could clearly hear them impersonating her. She rolled her eyes. She had taken Latin for under a year at her previous school. Honestly, languages came fairly easy to her. Had she wanted to actually show off, she probably could've. That wasn't Lena's way though. She preferred to fly under the radar. No need to form unnecessary class competition or gain unnecessary attention. She decided to let the comments slide for now.

The teacher was going on about different language types. "Dead Language" was now written on the board and underlined about five too many times. In an attempt to make a friend, Lena tilted to the person next to her. "If Latin is such a dead language, I wonder if only the dead speak it?" She smiled and let out a giggle. They, however, did not. If anything, they were a little freaked out. "It's just a joke. Relax." Lena couldn't tell if it was in her head or not, but she swore they moved their desk further away from her after that. Why was everyone so sensitive here?

Returning her focus to class, she reached for her pencil. Out of nowhere, it flew from her grasp, hitting the person in front of her. They turned with a scowl. Wide-eyed, Lena mouthed a profuse apology. This day was going down in the books as the worst first day ever. The group from before was now laughing so hard that they drew the attention of Mr. Babel. He was thrilled to have their participation. Their faces indicated they were not. One even shot a dirty look directly towards Lena. Time could not pass soon enough for her.

Lena studied her schedule. Practice was next, then lunch. *What am I supposed to practice? I haven't joined anything.* She had no idea where to go next. She hoped she could find a quiet place to be alone. As usual, a crowd amassed at the first sound of the bell. Remembering Simon's advice, Lena let everyone go ahead. When she rose to leave, she only made it two steps before falling face first onto the hard linoleum floor.

"OW!" She sat up in time to see two kids high-five on their way out the door. There was nothing in front of her. *Did I trip over air?*

Mr. Babel extended his hand. "Sorry about them. Not everyone here has the best manners. Are you okay?"

Lena was doing everything not to cry. "I'm fine. Thank you. What's high school without a few pranks, right?" She tried to laugh it off.

Mr. Babel wasn't buying it. "If it happens again, you can always come to me. I'll make sure it's handled." He sounded so different than during his lesson; all his excitement was replaced with seriousness.

"I'm sure it'll be fine." Lena could feel wetness trickle below her nose. Fists clenched, she wiped her face. "Can you point me to the closest restroom please?" He obliged and escorted her out.

She dashed into the bathroom, snatched some paper towels for her bloody nose, and darted for the stall furthest from the door. Tears started pouring the second the lock clicked in place. The stall was spacious. Lena found a bench and curled into it. Soundless sobs shook her body. She nestled into the corner and there she stayed as her classes passed.

~~~~~~~~~~~~~~~~~~~~~~~~~~~~~~~

There was a soft knock at the door. "Hello?"

Lena sniffled. "Uh, hi. I'll be done in a minute, okay?" It dawned on her that this was probably an accessible stall. She chided herself for blocking out someone in need.

"Oh, no. I don't need to come in. I felt…. Well, I got notified, I guess … that something might be wrong. You've been in there for a while now." The girl trailed off. "My name is Airess. Can I help get you to the nurse?"

Might as well, Lena figured. Reluctantly, she opened the door. Airess' hair was bubble gum pink and her grin was just as bright. She was strikingly beautiful. Lena couldn't help but smile back. "Hi, I'm Lena."

Airess reached out and gave her a big hug. "I was so worried!"

"You don't even know me."

"You don't have to know someone to be worried about their well-being, silly. What happened?" Airess assessed Lena's welfare tactfully.

"Nothing I can't handle. A few kids were just being jerks."

"Does it hurt?" Airess touched her own nose reflexively.

Lena stole a short glance in the mirror. Her nose was bruised and twice its normal size. "I'll be fine." She rubbed it compulsively.

"You sound like a friend of mine. They rarely take help either. Too late for you though! Let's go to

the nurse! She's expecting us."
Airess wrapped her arm in Lena's
and they headed out the door.

It felt nice to have someone be
so kind-hearted and comforting,
stranger or not. Airess' positivity
was contagious. She was so chirpy
and bouncy. The whole walk, she
leaned into Lena whispering like
they were best friends. *So this is
what that feels like*, Lena thought.

"Here we are! And look! Solei! I
was just talking about you, friend!"
Airess hopped to boop Simon's
head.

Lena gave a small wave.
"Simon?" she verified.

"Oh, hey! You're the lost girl
from this morning. Lost and hurt,

huh? Lucky da—Yikes! That hurt, Airess! How do you know I'm not here for a broken shin bone? You could've hospitalized me!" Simon yelped dramatically.

"Be nice. Plus, you'd tell me you'd just walk it off anyway. I will not be guilt-tripped with your stubbornness." Airess gave a full smile.

"You kids cause quite a ruckus!" A nurse came rolling out from behind a partition. "Solei, what a lucky surprise." She signaled Simon towards an empty cot then turned towards Lena. "And you, pet? I'm not sure I recognize you. I'm Ms. Galen. I'm the nurse here at Legacy Academy." She took hold of Lena's chin. "Why don't you take a seat? I need to see if that's broken. Airess, can you please set up Solei with an electric blanket while I take a look at our friend's nose here?"

"Sure thing! I'll grab an ice pack for Lena too!"

"Quite the bump you've got there. Rough day on the training ground?" The nurse gently applied pressure and waved her hand over Lena's face.

"Training ground? No. I tripped over air because that's how today's been. It's been the best first day ever." Lena's sarcasm was evident.

"Things are rarely nothing here, but you, my dear, are good to go!" A timer dinged behind them.

"That means you're done too!" Airess removed the blanket off Simon. "It's almost time for last period. Want to go to the courtyard together?"

"Definitely! How about you, little cub?" Simon playfully kicked Lena's chair.

"Oh. Me? I … umm … I don't know what my last class is. I'll look!" Lena began rummaging in her bag.

Airess came over and put her hand on top of Lena's. "Everyone has a study hall as their last period of the day. You go wherever is best for you to focus. Solei likes being outside as long as it isn't rainy. I'm happy anywhere there are people. What best fits your element?"

"My element?"

"Yeah, what's your talent based on?" Airess was fluttering in anticipation. "Do you teleport, or make fire, or heal people? I'm a healer! I love it!"

Simon was trying to pull Airess aside; they could see alarm overtaking Lena. "Airess, I don't think she knows."

"Knows?" Airess didn't understand.

"Knows what?" both girls asked in unison.

Simon handed Lena a mirror. Instinctively, she raised it to look at her nose. Her face was perfect, not a blemish to be seen. No bruises, no cuts, not even any acne. Her skin was smooth and clear. She looked at her two classmates sitting across from her. "What's going on?"

Airess wouldn't meet Lena's gaze. She looked sad, almost apologetic. The bell sounded. Simon stood. "Come on, little cub. I think we need to introduce you to your new school." They picked up Lena's bag and handed it to her. Airess sulked behind Simon.

"This is all getting too bizarre. I should just go." Lena scrambled to leave.

"If you can't handle us in here, I'm not quite sure how you're going to survive out there." Simon pulled the door open.

Lena watched as the large herd of students pushed by. At first, the scene appeared perfectly normal, but as she concentrated on each individual instead of the large mass, she began to notice things. A flickering of light in someone's eyes. *Was that a flame?* A girl who didn't seem to be touching the ground. *She couldn't be flying, could she?* Another whose eyes were a solid abyss of black. That couldn't be right. She had to be seeing things. She felt a light touch upon her hand.

"I'm so sorry, Lena. I had no idea you didn't know. I think it's really irresponsible to send you here without letting you know what you're getting into. Can I try to help?" Airess' doe eyes watered. Lena nodded in a daze. Her fear instantly started to subside; she squeezed Airess' hand reflexively. Airess didn't let go, she added her other hand on top as they stood up together. Simon put their arm around Lena.

"Welcome to Legacy Academy, little cub." As Simon gestured to the hallway in front of them, it was almost as if small golden sparks illuminated their words.

~~~~~~~~~~~~~~~~~~~~~~~~~~~~~~

Legacy Academy. Where everyone is, well, a legacy. Now, someone floored by this information may repetitively ask "Legacy of what?" The answer? Of gods. Legacies. Of. Gods.

What?! "WE'RE ALL RELATED TO GODS?!" Lena was still screaming her newfound facts at Tao.

"Related or chosen. Hey, can you please tone it down? You're acting absurdly and it's giving me a headache." He postulated Lena may be the most draining person he'd ever met, and last year he'd had a class with a succubus.

"I'M THE ONE ACTING ABSURDLY?! I JUST GOT TOLD I'M ATTENDING A SCHOOL FULL OF GODS—WHICH INCLUDES ME BY THE WAY!"

"You, Lena Basil, are not a god." He paused for that to sink in. "That said, I am in agreement that someone probably should have told you." He shrugged, holding open the door for her.

"Yeah! Someone should have! Where was that in all your tours? Maybe next time, instead of showing me the city hall and police station combo, YOU TELL ME I'M RELATED TO GODS!" Lena slammed the door behind her.

Tao got into the driver's seat. "One: We don't know if you're biologically related or not. Two: That is probably the responsibility of someone involved in your life and not the boy paid to take you to the store." He watched for her reaction as he pulled out of his parking spot; she sat paralyzed. "I'm sorry. I didn't mean that to sound so harsh. You're clearly having a rough day."

You have no idea.

"How about you tell me everything that happened on our way to your house and I'll try to fill in the blanks where I can? I'm in a state of shock too. I've never met a student so blindsided before."

Lena stared out the window. "Does everyone know who they belong to but me?" she whispered.

"Mostly. Even if they don't know the god they're affiliated with, they know the general basis for their talents or their family's lineage. That's usually a huge part of their upbringing."

Her parents had never really talked about their extended family before and Lena had never thought to ask. She knew her parents were both only children and that her grandparents had passed years before she was born. Their family was always the three of them. Sure, they sometimes talked of their African and Egyptian roots over the years, but never in a "Hey, you see that sphinx over there? That's your Great Aunt Clara!" or "See that sarcophagus? Wave hi to Grandpa!" kind of way. This was all too overwhelming for Lena.

Tao knocked on the passenger window. He had all her bags from the store ready to go. "Listen, I'm sure whatever reason your family has is a valid one, but if you need someone to talk to, I'm around. My only requirement is no more yelling." He put his business card in her hand.

"A business card? Really? What are you? Forty?" She stopped. "Wait, don't answer that. I've been told too many weird things today and I don't want that to be another. Also, thanks."

"I imagine what you heard from Airess and Solei will take some time to process."

"Hey! One last thing," Lena called out. "Why do some people call Simon 'Simon' and some people call them 'Solei'?"

Tao let out a full belly laugh. "Now that sounds like a typical first day question from a new Legacy student. That's better answered by them and not me."

Lena had anticipated that was going to be the case. "Thanks, Tao."

"Anytime Lena." He tapped the hood of his car and drove away.

Unsure of what to do next, she wandered around outside. Lena knew she needed to talk to her parents, but what would she say? *Hey Mom and Dad, want to know what I learned on my first day at school? That you've been lying to me my whole life and I'm the kin of some random god that may or may not have any relation to what I believed my heritage to be for the last fourteen years of my life.* Lena stared at her front door. Then she glanced down the street to see the

Old Hag's house. For a second, she imagined how horribly wrong that could've gone, knowing what she knew now. No wonder Tao didn't follow her in, or those bullies for that matter. There were two layers to the world Lena saw now. It was time to go in.

"Mom! Dad! I'm home!" Lena waited for a response. When none came, she headed up to her room. Her door was slightly ajar and she could hear a voice muttering inside. "Mom?"

"Magdalena! How are you? How was your first day?"

Lena gazed around her room. There were socks everywhere, all clustered in groups of similar colors and descending in similar sizes. "What are you doing in here?"

"Oh! I thought some extra organization might be good for your first day! I gathered all the socks in the house and I'm putting them in tied-up bundles in your drawers!" Kamilah seemed so proud of herself.

Lena picked up the sock closest to her. "I don't think this is mine. And why are you tying them up in bundles?" Her mom had started to hum, barely listening to Lena, as she cut and tied the twine.

"Mom?" Lena was struggling to get through to her mother. "Where's Dad?"

Kamilah shook her head and went back to work.

"No! You're not going to ignore me right now!" Lena ripped the socks from her mother's hands and grabbed her by the shoulders. "Where is my dad?!"

Kamilah's tears were instantaneous. Once she couldn't reach her project anymore, she fixated on to Lena's angry eyes and scurried away. Lena retracted her grip the moment she saw her mother's fright, but it was too hard to mask her frustration. Her mom was hysterical now and confined within Lena's empty closet. Kamilah let out ear-piercing howls in between her shaky breathing. Her only uttered words were a repeated track of, "I don't know, I don't know, I don't know."

Desperate, Lena texted her dad and set off to find her mother's calming blanket. She ran from room to room but only found stacks of unopened boxes. She had just resigned herself to having to open them one by one when her dad burst through the front door.

"Mags! I'm here! Where is she?"

"Up here! She's in my bedroom." Her dad was immediately by her mom's side, reassuring Kamilah's safety with his every step. Kasim reached out for his wife, luring her into his arms. Upon finding his warmth, she collapsed into him. The angst in the room eased. Kasim stroked his wife's hair and kissed the top of her head.

"I'm sorry, Magpie. It had to be nerve-racking coming home and seeing her like this."

"No. It wasn't—"

"Something about socks, it looks like?"

"She was organizing them and tying them in bundles. They weren't even mine."

He picked up one near him that looked like his size and lifted it to his nose. "Or clean." He grimaced in a funny way, tossing the sock over to Lena, making her bat at it. Her dad always handled these situations so much better than she did.

"I'm going to take your mom to lie down. I'll clean this up later. Why don't you go do some homework or explore the town a bit?" Lena had no homework since she had hidden in the bathroom for half the day and had no desire to spend any more time in Astoria.

"Sure thing, Dad."

"That's my girl."

Lena laid down on her bed, peering out her window. This. This was why Lena had no idea what was going on in the world around her. How were her parents supposed to explain deities and supreme beings to her when her mom couldn't even hold a conversation? Not to mention all the clean up her dad had to do after every breakdown. *It's not fair.*

Deflated, Lena collected the socks in her room and took them down to the wash. She re-examined her family's statues while she waited, wondering if there were secret messages behind the items she always took for granted. Lena carried the socks upstairs when they were done and sorted them by owner. She put hers away first and on the way to deliver the rest to her parents, she noticed the twine and scissors were still on the floor. She placed those in the laundry basket too after tying her mom's socks together in a bundle. She knocked on their bedroom door.

"Come in." Her mom's voice was faint and airy.

"I brought these up, fresh from the dryer."

"How sweet of you, Lena. Go ahead and put them in the dresser, if you don't mind."

"Not a problem."

Her dad walked into the room as Lena was putting the socks away.

"Hey, can I ask a question?" Lena's nerves were welling in her belly.

"Anything at all." Her dad looked over.

"At school today, I heard some ... things. I was curious to know if they were true." Her mom was puzzled. Everyone looked to Kasim.

"Ah. I probably should've expected that. Go ahead, Lena."

"It's just.... I heard.... It sounds so crazy saying it out loud." Lena could feel her cheeks redden.

"Things that seem normal to me sound crazy out loud all the time," Kamilah said with conviction.

Lena stifled a laugh. "I heard a rumor today that Legacy was a school for people who shared a connection with the gods. That has to be nuts, right? Especially since, I imagine, if we were godly descendants you would've told me that."

"Of course we would've told you that, sweetheart. I wouldn't have been able to keep something like that from you." Her father's tone was factual.

The knot in Lena's stomach loosened. She felt relieved. "So, the girls, they were making it up?"

His face strained. "Not exactly."

"What do you mean?"

"I mean we don't believe we share a bloodline with any gods. That part is true. Nonetheless, Legacy is in fact a school for those who are chosen by gods or are related to them."

"If that's true, then why am I there?"

"Well, the short answer is since your mother and I are both alumni, you're allowed to attend as well. The long answer is slightly aspirational."

"Aspirational?" *What does that even mean?*

"Yes, your mother and I, both are Legacies. We were chosen by different gods and we hope the same for you."

"I want to make sure I understand this correctly. You're telling me that I go to a magical school with all these other kids, who likely have super awesome great-grandparents, and my best bet is hoping some cosmic being thinks I'm cool—eventually?"

Her father's tone got terse. "Don't be disrespectful, Lena. You are correct, though, that you have not been chosen yet."

"And I'm not related to Zeus or any Zeus-like figures?"

"Zeus." Her mother stuck her tongue out.

Kasim chuckled. "That is also true and we should be grateful for that. The Greek line can get messy at times." He said this earnestly, but it didn't ebb his daughter's frustration.

Lena groaned with exasperation. "I'm going to bed, family. Good night."

"Hey Lena?" her mom said softly. Lena turned to acknowledge

her. "Why did you tie my socks in a bundle? It's cute, but isn't that a little counterproductive?"

"No reason, Mom. No reason at all." Lena shut her parents' door behind her, disheartened.

Chapter 4

Textbooks and Talents

Lena was silent on the ride to school. She had so many questions but nothing to say. She hoped if she ignored the day before, life would go back to normal. When she got out of the car, she kept her eyes locked on the ground. Her goal was to avoid everyone and everything. Upon opening her locker, she was surprised to see it was full of textbooks. There was a familiar looking note hanging down from the top shelf.

"Dear Miss Basil,

I anticipate this finds you well. It occurred to me, after our meeting, that you have not been provided with your much-needed materials. I apologize greatly for my oversight and hope that the search for them was not too derailing from yesterday's scheduled activities. Your professors have all been assured that the blame for your many absences rests solely on my shoulders and I will rectify my actions post-haste! You will now be able to attend your lessons, qualms resolved. I look forward to your instructors' confirmation that I have righted my error.

All my best on your first day of classes,

Principal Chromwell

P.S. I have attached another schedule for you.

P.P.S. I hope your nose continues to feel better."

"She is nothing if not informed, I guess," Lena murmured underneath her breath.

"She's kind of like Santa Claus. P.C. knows and sees all, and it's not even her super power," Tao interjected. Simon and Airess stood to his side.

"Morning, little cub."

"Hi!" Airess leaped in for a big hug. It seemed to be directed only at Lena, but Tao got wrapped up in it too.

"What are you guys doing here? You all know each other?" Lena hadn't expected that.

"Tao and I grew up here together." Simon nudged him.

"I moved here a few years back. Solei was my first friend too!" Airess bounced back over to Simon.

"You have a type, huh Simon?" Lena teased playfully as she closed her locker.

They chuckled. "Fresh meat, little cub! What can I say? But the important question is where are we headed off to this morning?"

"Umm..." Lena took out her schedule. "Illusions, Apparitions, and Mirages is my first period."

"That's clear across campus. My first period is only a few hallways down..." Tao whined. Airess kicked him subtly. "But anything for my new friend."

Lena eyed them. "I don't need any special treatment. I'll manage."

"We're friends now! Friends help each other!" Airess tapped a finger on her nose as she spoke. "Hey! I think that's Kohl's class!" A look of agreement passed over Simon and Tao.

"Who's Kohl?" Lena asked.

"Another new friend! Let's go!" In typical Airess fashion, off they went, arm in arm.

~~~~~~~~~~~~~~~~~~~~~~~~~~~~

Tao wasn't wrong; the trek from Lena's locker to her first class was quite the hike. Lena hated to admit that it would've been nearly impossible to figure out by herself. Legacy was overrun with twists and turns. Nothing about the school felt innate to Lena.

"Found it! Now let's find Kohl!" Airess left to search for him.

Lena scanned the room. There was, unfortunately, one face she recognized. It was the student she had tried to befriend the previous day, the one that moved their desk as far away as they could from her.

"KOHL!" Simon bellowed. Everyone looked at them. "If he's in there, he'll have heard me."

The only face Lena recognized stood up.

"No, no, no, no, no...." She cowered behind Tao.

"Yay! You're here!" Airess gleamed. "Kohl meet Lena, Lena meet Kohl!"

"Hello." His voice was steady and oddly soothing. Lena peeked over Tao's shoulder. "Oh." By the look on his face, Kohl recognized her too.

"Hi," she squeaked.

"Lena?" Tao stepped aside.

She tried to pull him back. "We've met. He hates me."

"Whatever happened, it's not that bad, Lena," reassured Simon.

"It might be." Kohl ran his fingers through his hair, offering a nervous smile. "She asked if only the dead speak Latin after having spoken Latin."

Airess gaped. "We all make mistakes! I'm sure you'll find a different topic today!" She ushered Lena and Kohl into class together. "I promise, no more talks of ghosts or Latin." Lena could hear the apprehension in her friend's voice.

Resigned, Kohl claimed a place for both of them to sit. Lena turned to wave goodbye to the others before taking her seat

Class was pretty uneventful. This teacher was nothing like Mr. Babel. His voice was stale and monotone, minus one major exception. To regain attention, he'd yell random onomatopoeias at unsuspecting students. Lena assumed very few illusions went "BAM!" or that many mirages went "SNAP!" Nevertheless, after yesterday, Lena decided it best not to judge.

"Wanna walk to our languages class together after this?" Kohl asked.

Smoke swirled deep within the color of his eyes. They were

mesmerizing. She couldn't drop her gaze. "That would be great."

"WHOOSH! Apparitions often disappear as swiftly as they appear." The teacher interrupted the moment. Karmically, the bell rang.

Lena stayed close to Kohl as they walked. Mr. Babel's class was, thankfully, fairly ordinary. In between lectures, Kohl told her that their grade level had practice, lunch, and study hall during the same block of time. Lena was excited to be with her newfound friends so often.

"Have you grown up here with Tao and Simon too or are you newer, like Airess and me?"

"I've been here since I was young, but I fade in and out. Legacy isn't always for me."

"Oh." Lena felt sad at the possibility of losing a friend so quickly. "How come?"

"Legacy is extraordinary at helping kids figure out how to be their true selves, but what if that's not what someone wants? What if what someone wants is to be less of themself instead of more?" Kohl posed longingly. "Not every talent feels like a gift. Sometimes, it feels more like a curse." An awkward silence stayed between them until the end of class.

Lena suspected she had an idea of what was going on but wasn't ready to say it aloud. The entrance to the courtyard was blinding. The sun's glare burned her eyes. She held on to Kohl to let him navigate.

"Mind if I crash the party?" he asked.

"You mean join the party! And—DUH! ¡Mi mesa es tu mesa! Welcome to practice!" Airess bubbled.

"You speak Spanish, Airess?" Lena loved the idea of sharing languages with someone.

"No, she's just a profound listener," Tao responded.

"And a good copycat!" ragged Simon.

"It sounds like you do though? And Latin?" Kohl quizzed.

"I know a little about a lot of things, but languages come easier than most. What are we practicing? Do I get to see everyone's talents?" Lena asked enthusiastically.

"That's kind of a personal question, Lena. What someone can do, and what god they're affiliated with, is really exclusive to them. Divulging all of that could leave someone highly vulnerable," Tao explained defensively.

"Mhmm, it's absolutely everyone's best-kept secret and not broadcasted publicly by their cliques at all." Simon motioned to the various social clusters around the courtyard.

Lena noticed a majority of the groups shared similar physical features with one another, yet one in particular caught her eye. On top of an adjacent table sat three identical fair-skinned girls, each were adorned with golden leaves pinned into their hair.

"The oracles," Kohl chimed in. "That whole group claims to be of Greek lineage. The ones with the golden bay leaves say they're actual oracles."

"And, therefore, feel they're more important than everyone else." Simon guffawed.

"I thought Apollo only had one oracle at a time?" Lena asked. "And that he was kind of infamous for getting thrown out of Olympus," she added in a low voice.

Tao had never appeared so happy. "That, my friend, is how we know it is all made-up nonsense."

"That he only had one oracle? Or that they're all oracles?" Lena was uncertain.

"Can't it be both? None of this is based on any sort of proof," Tao replied.

"That's not true; I've seen the rings light up quite a few times," Airess interjected.

"The rings?" Lena was losing track of the conversation.

"No one sees anything in the rings. It's not like they glow and Papa Legba pops up from the ground and gives you a big hug." Tao rolled his eyes.

"It'd do you well to have more faith in what you can't see, Tao Vovi." Airess glanced from Tao to Kohl and back.

"It'd do you well to be impressed with what's right in front of you, Goddess." The brutish twins flanked Airess out of nowhere. Their skin was a disgusting shade of green and their teeth looked sharpened. "Hey newbie. Legacy or Descendant?"

"That doesn't make any sense to me," Lena countered.

"Ha! Probably a Legacy then. I should've guessed from your friends here. An encyclopedia, a chicken, someone who refuses to see what's good for her, and a big giant question mark. If you knew what was good for you, you'd find better chums to be around. You'll be nothing with these losers."

"I'd happily spend time with a flock of chickens before engaging in your aroma. What is that? Decay? Livestock manure? Please, if I agree to be a loser forever, will you agree to use some soap and maybe some bath salts?" Lena implored.

"Oink, oink, loser. Takes a pig to smell one!" One of them threw a piece of jerky at Lena before going to sit with the oracles. Tao snatched it up.

"Never accept food here." He threw it out. "The Academy cafeteria should be your only source of outside food. You never know where something else here has come from."

"How'd you know they helped with the animals on campus here, little cub?" Simon asked cautiously.

"The plants too, they help grow the crops from the animal droppings. That's where I frequently run into them," Airess concurred.

"Fantastic insights, really, but the lunchroom is opening up and I want to be first. Come on." Tao convinced Simon and Airess to go grab food with him.

Lena pulled out snacks from her bag.

"Lena." Kohl was staring at his hands.

"Yeah Kohl?"

"How did you know that they smelled like decay?"

"I don't know. It's a pretty distinctive smell. The green skin helped too, I guess. Why?" She opened her bag of chips.

"Their green skin?" He had a grave expression on his face.

"And pointy teeth! They looked straight out of a fairy tale."

"Lena." Kohl's voice sounded grim.

"Yes?" *How many times is he going to say my name like that?*

"They don't have green skin. Not until night-time anyway." He discreetly took a picture of the twins and showed it to her.

Lena was silent. She looked back and forth. On the phone were two pale, buff, buzzcut football players. In front of her were two sloppy, dirty, chartreuse tinted heathens.

"What is this?" Lena could feel her panic rising.

"This is a cell phone. That, however, is a ghoul, a busaw, actually. They're ghouls no one else can see while there's daylight out."

Lena pushed Kohl's phone back to him and fainted.

~~~~~~~~~~~~~~~~~~~~~~~~~~~~~~~~~~~~~

Lena's vision was hazy when she woke up. Her sight went from pitch black to blindingly bright. She could feel someone squeeze her hand as she stirred.

"Are you okay? What happened?" There was compassion in Simon's voice.

"Yay! You're up! When we came back from the cafeteria, you were passed out! You're lucky Kohl caught you!" Airess buzzed.

"I remember we were on Kohl's phone and ..." Lena's eyes caught Kohl fervently waving his hand across his neck in a nixing manner. "And that's it, I guess?"

"Maybe she's sensitive to the sun," Simon suggested.

"Or being thrown into Legacy is too much for her," Tao stated confidently. Lena glowered at him. "What? I meant it nicely."

"Never mind him. I think you need some rest. You haven't been unconscious long, so we have some time. You're a pro at skipping class at this point!" Airess went to clear the room. "I'll be back in a bit!"

This space was different from the nurse's office. The walls were stark white and there were lights everywhere. Lena couldn't find the entrance or the exit.

"Back! Sorry! I wanted to get them out of here." Airess re-entered.

"It's fine. What is this place?"

"Oh! Yeah! Welcome to Ward B! It's our school infirmary. It also serves as the town hospital. We function as an all-in-one around here!"

"It's huge."

"Yeah, we can fit all of Astoria in here if needed." She was mixing some type of salve. "This will help with your headache. It should reorient you too." Airess held her breath for a moment. "Hey Lena?"

The last time someone said her name like that, she passed out. "Yeah Airess?"

"You know I'm a healer, right?"

"Of course. Why?"

"Healers can solve physical ailments easily; it's what we're best known for." She glopped the salve onto Lena's forehead. "I imagine you don't know we're blessed with other talents too. Healers can typically feel emotions in their surroundings. It's how I knew you were in the bathroom; I could feel your pain. I knew you were in distress." Airess paused, rubbing in the medicine. "And when I make physical contact with people, it increases the intensity of my talents tenfold." Lena averted her eyes. "I'm not a mind reader and I'm not going to force you to tell me what happened. Nonetheless, it's very hard to care for a patient without knowing the full story. Does that make sense?" Lena agreed, avoiding eye contact. Airess waited a few minutes to see if Lena would give her any insight into what happened.

She didn't. "Ms. Galen should be around shortly to check on you."

"Hey, see you during study hall?"

"I'll be around." Airess' voice was distant. Lena knew she had let her down, but Kohl's actions were explicit. She hated being stuck in the middle of something she didn't understand. She couldn't wait to sort everything out.

Ms. Galen didn't keep Lena waiting. She held Lena's head, checked her eyes, and sent her on her way. It was seventh period, the second to last of the day. Lena retrieved the map out of her backpack and went to leave. Her hand was on the door to go.

"STOP!"

Lena jumped back, startled.

"Where do you think you're going?!" Airess was furious. She was rushing towards Lena with vigor. Ms. Galen came into view too. It felt unreal to see Airess in such a rage. *What have I done now?*

Lena's chest was tightening. She couldn't speak.

Ms. Galen stepped between the girls.

"I'll take it from here, pet. Why don't you go check on our other residents? I'll help Ms. Basil." Airess had been dismissed. Ms. Galen hugged Lena. "It's okay. Let me see what you've got there." The nurse studied the map from Principal

Chromwell. It was turned around; the school was on the other side of the room. "Ope! Here we go. All straightened out." She handed it back to Lena.

"Why was she so mad? What did I do?" Lena was heaving and shaking.

"There, there. You and Airess are both good girls. She tends to feel all her emotions very strongly. And you ... you're new to learning. You both need to have some patience. Life's going to be bumpy for a while." Ms. Galen gave one last squeeze. "Think you'll make it?"

Lena nodded. "I wish I knew what I did or knew what was wrong. I didn't think I could mess up by simply going to class."

Ms. Galen's heart ached. "You head to class and I'll talk to Airess, deal? I'm sure it's all a misunderstanding."

Lena sniffled in agreement.

"You're losing your touch, Galen!" a man taunted from a nearby bed. Lena couldn't make out his figure. Her view was too blurry. "You sendin' girls back when they're almost walking into walls after you heal them? I knew you'd fail sooner or later." Lena went to say something, but Ms. Galen blocked her view.

"To class, Ms. Basil. I can manage the rest."

"Yes, ma'am." She glanced at her map one last time and followed it to the school building next door.

Lena arrived at her locker to switch out her textbooks when she caught a wisp out of the corner of her eye.

"Hey," Kohl said.

Lena was a powder keg of emotions ready to burst. "Hey?! I hope you have a lot more than 'hey' for all the trouble you caused!"

"Trouble that I caused?"

"Yes! I saw your theatrical show in the infirmary, so I didn't tell anybody what happened, and then Airess lost her mind on me! First she was sad; then she was out-of-her-mind livid! I'm really trying my best here, but I feel like I'm in some type of tug of war between you two and I can't take it!"

"I had no idea. Maybe I should've thought that through more. I'm sorry. I'd like to explain if you'll let me?"

Lena was still angry. She kept her arms crossed but let him lead her a few lockers down.

"Do you see me?"

"Don't waste my time, Kohl." Her irritation was peaking.

"There, do you see me there?" Kohl remained calm and pointed to his reflection.

"Yes. Why are we doin—"

"How about now?"

Lena watched the mirror he pointed at. She only saw herself. She looked at him and the fear started to set in again.

He put his hands up. "Don't freak out. It's all better now."

She glanced over and there his reflection was.

"One more time. What do you see in my hand?"

This time, Lena looked into the mirror first, nothing. She focused on his hand. "I see a cloud. Maybe some lightning?" Lena closed her eyes to calm down then reopened them. She could hear rain. She felt thunder. "It's a storm." It vanished. Kohl was incredibly impressed.

"What you see in the mirror, Lena Basil, is what the rest of us see. What you see in front of you is typically something only the user can see."

"I can't make mini hand storms or become invisible. I've tried doing that before I knew anything about Legacy." She hesitated. "Wait, I'm not going to turn green like those disgusting twins, am I?"

Kohl was amused with Lena. "No. You don't have our powers. Listen, I'm not an expert, that's more Tao's thing, but I think I know your power, Lena. I also want to preface this by saying the reason I urged you to keep quiet at the hospital was because I didn't want you to expose yourself without knowing it. The only people who should have this kind of information are the people you choose to share it with." He took a deep breath. "Lena, I think what you have is referred to as True Sight."

"Oh." She had thought this moment would feel more ... momentous. Or clarifying. It wasn't either. "That was very thoughtful, I guess." Lena tried to come up with more to say. "What do I do now?"

The hallways started to fill. "That is completely up to you, Miss Basil. I, however, have practice to skip." Kohl turned to mist right before her eyes.

"Helpful," Lena scoffed.

~~~~~~~~~~~~~~~~~~~~~~~~~~~~~~~~

Practice had been vapid. Lena sat distanced from the group to begin with; then, when Airess arrived, Airess mimicked the same behavior in the opposite direction. Lena's heart weighed heavily every time her friend ignored her. She missed Airess' hugs already, even if part of her now questioned the reasoning behind them. Lena blocked out the noise around her. She tried to use her new proposed talent. The world was left unchanged. Tired of the pang in her heart, she left to walk home.

Lena wanted to talk to her dad. She wanted to ask him every question about herself, and her family, that could possibly be created. She searched the house and his workspace for him to no avail. Defeated, once again, Lena retreated to her computer upstairs.

She had so much to research. Hours were dedicated to "True Sight" and "Latin" and "Apparitions." The internet didn't offer any revelations. While engrossed in one rabbit hole of information, an article listed the best way to tell if you're interacting with a ghost is to pass a hand through them. Amused by daydreams of poking an intangible Kohl to check his solidity, Lena fell fast asleep.

Chapter 5

Distress and Disaster

Lena woke to the vibration of her phone. School alerts filled her notifications.

"Courtyard closed until further notice."

"Students: urgent request to check in for safety."

"Residents are urged to return to their dorms."

"Classes to be determined. Please click here for more information."

Lena pulled out Tao's business card and texted him straight away.

He responded within seconds. "I'll pick you up."

Lena presumed the entire school must be on edge. *What happened? In a school full of godly legacies, it could be anything! Does this happen often? I have to see this!*

A crowd packed the academy's expansive lawn. Groups were huddled together everywhere gossiping, each one looking to obtain new information before the others. Lena spotted Simon in their sports gear.

"There!" Lena pulled Tao towards the school's entrance.

"Little cub! What are you doing here?" There was a look of concern on Simon's face.

"Tao brought me! I couldn't miss this! What's going on?" Lena was high on adrenaline.

"I'm surprised you came so late, Vovi; aren't you P.C.'s emergency standby?" Simon chaffed.

"Funny. You should go on tour with that humor. I'm sure your fans would find you electrifying. Hey!" He jumped, holding his shoulder. "Airess!" Tao yelled for the bubble gum schoolgirl.

She sprinted towards the group. Simon swept her up in a big hug. "I can't believe they kept you in there! What did you find?"

Airess' face was desolate. "A whole lot of nothing. No one can even get close."

"Close to what?" Lena reached for her friend's hand. Airess held Tao's then too.

Simon explained in distress, "When I was on the field practicing today, all I saw was a mist spreading out from the courtyard. A few teammates fell to the ground, but most of us got out. Chromwell locked the doors seconds later. That's when the notifications started coming. Everyone on this lawn came after. I was terrified for the people stuck inside. I couldn't believe P.C. didn't lift the cell signal blockade."

"Honestly, inside feels totally normal now. I had just finished a shift in Ward A when Ms. Galen left a message on my clipboard. She wanted me to meet her in Chromwell's office. Legacy was empty, but the time was so early I didn't think much of it. It wasn't until I was walking along the front entrance windows that I picked up on any residual fear. All the doors to the courtyard are expertly sealed. Whatever happened is highly contained, which is good. I tried to sneak a peek through the mist before Ms. Galen escorted me out.

All I could see was a thick fog."
Airess longed to be back inside.

"Ward A?" Lena asked. "Could you read the emotions from P.C. or Ms. Galen?"

"No. They were all business as usual." Airess felt half gone.

"What did they have you do when they called you to meet with them?" Tao had an idea.

"I went to the Headmistress' Chambers. They told me there had been an accident in the courtyard. I was asked if I had seen anything out of the ordinary. I hadn't. Then Ms. Galen gave me a small examination, a ginseng tablet, and escorted me out. I feel awful that

I'm of no help. I should be on the front line with them."

"Hey, was that tablet yellow and bitter?" Simon inquired. "They brought out a funny smelling drink a while ago and I was curious what it was."

"Usually. The ones we use have sugar in them, so they're not that bad. Most people believe it helps restore balance." Airess' concentration reminded Lena of her mom.

"I think that's the tea they brought out for us earlier." Simon pointed to a table of snacks and a giant yellow pitcher. "I want to check."

The doors of Legacy Academy swung open. An airy cloud billowed out the door. Principal Chromwell emerged with a small entourage trailing behind her. Lena recognized some of them. One was Ms. Galen and other was definitely Kasim Basil.

"Dad?!" Lena hollered. His eyes got stern. They both knew she was not supposed to be here.

"Lena, Kasim is your dad?" Simon's jaw dropped.

"Good morning, students. I appreciate your fine temperaments as we process today's events together. A large mishap has come our way, but worry not! My most trusted peers are dedicated to a resolution! During these hours of uncertainty, please excuse yourselves to your own residences. I am eager to be in touch with you all shortly. Au revoir, my children, stay vigilant!" As abruptly as Legacy's leader appeared, she left.

Lena tried to run to her father. He held out his hand in protest and retreated into the building. Ms. Galen approached the group.

"Ms. Hikona, Mr. Vovi, your presence is being requested." Airess and Tao obeyed without response.

Lena was in shock. "My DAD is in there and they choose them?!"

"It's because of their gifts, Lena. You can't expect them to invite a student who hasn't honed their skills yet. Anyways, side note, I can't believe Kasim is your dad! How did you not know you were touched by gods with him as a parent? He's beyond famous!" Simon's increased volume was attracting spectators.

"Let's go where people can't hear us, Simon."

"I have just the place!" Their eyes lit in illumination.

~~~~~~~~~~~~~~~~~~~~~~~~~~~~~~

"You're going to kill us! We're going to die!" Lena wailed.

"No, we're not. Keep climbing. Watch out for that antennae."

Lena's foot slipped and she clenched the metal frame. "I'm going to die!"

"Little cub. Stop it. Open your eyes, put one foot above the other, avoid giant pieces of metal, and get up on this platform."

Electricity crackled all around Lena. "Next time, we're going somewhere normal!" She mounted the stairs.

"This is my favorite spot in the whole world. This is where I feel most like a god." Their voice was solemn.

Lena sat cautiously beside Simon. "That might be the effects of radiation...."

"Perhaps." Simon wiggled their fingers as sparks hopped from one to the next.

"You're electric!" Lena was hyped with excitement.

"Easy there, don't fall." Simon shielded their cub. "My current has a vast array of utilities, but saving someone from a fifty-foot fall is not a feature."

"That might be the first thing that's made sense to me since I've gotten to Astoria. Is it rude if I ask you what you can do?"

"I wouldn't have brought you here to keep you in the dark." Simon winked.

"Punny too."

"Very! I like to think it's my greatest gift. Alas, manipulating electricity will have to do." Simon shot a miniscule firework into the air. "I want to talk about something much more astonishing. Your father! You live with a legend! How could you not share that, little cub?"

"That's an easy question to answer. I had no idea." Lena's expression was smug. "Let me help you with the list of facts I know about my dad: He is the world's greatest father, probably a better husband, and he enjoys woodwork. Unless his claim to fame is being able to list every species of wood, my surprise at seeing him today rivals your own."

"Come over sometime. I have stacks of books on the creation of magical items. Most of them highlight your dad. I always hoped he would write his own publication someday. Of all the things, you really didn't know he made P.C.'s staff? That type of finesse isn't even in the realm of possibilities for anyone else."

Lena remembered noticing the woodwork and thinking it was beyond her dad's skillset. "Nope. Not a single, solitary clue. It's a strong trend lately. I don't recommend it."

"I can't fathom how impossible this must be for you." Simon sent a zap down a thick wire. "If you want, you can call me Solei. It almost means 'sun' in French. My parents were ambitious about my powers when I was younger."

"So your name is Solei! Is Simon a nickname then?"

"The name Simon caught on once I started at Legacy. Since I didn't fit into societal norms, kids made fun of me for being dumb. 'Simple Simon' was their favorite slur. They'd chant it relentlessly. It wasn't true, but I preferred that to other options. I've been introducing myself as Simon ever since."

"That's horrible! How could the adults stand by and let them do that?! That's completely unacceptable!" Lena's anger was unmistakable.

"Because I asked them to, Lena. I bet that letting the bullies win that battle would save me from others. It worked." Simon's tone sounded remorseful.

Lena clutched her friend's hand. "I will never, NEVER, call you Simon again. That breaks my heart. If I had any inclination of the root of that name, I wouldn't have even considered that title as an option." She squeezed them tighter. "Your name is Solei."

"Don't make me cry. After all, water is a conductor." Solei bumped their friend. "Want to see what I can do?" Lena nodded. "I turned on a speaker within the school. We can listen in," Solei proudly informed her.

"Ingenious! How?" Excitement reigned in Lena again.

"A little bit of magic and a little bit of help on the inside." They held a sly grin.

"Tao?" Lena replayed the morning. "No. Airess! But when?"

"There are speakers hidden in plain sight around the school. I turn them on and Airess keeps them close by. The trick is that they have to be plugged in or I can't manipulate them. I need to share an unbroken circuit with whatever I'm connecting to."

"This tower links to almost the entire city." Lena gazed at the land below. "Wow!"

"Live in three ... two ... one ..." Solei amplified sound waves off a nearby satellite.

"You've had absolutely no premonitions, or insights, about the fog? You're sure, son?"

"I'm sorry, but, for the seventh time, no."

"It's useless, Kasim. We have no advantages here. Tao has had no visions. Nadea and Airess can heal pupils extracted from the mist, but there's no insight into the cause. Not to mention, even with combining their skills, they can't keep the rescue squads awake."

"My staff isn't able to clear the haze either and the mass absorbs any light cast into it. Our hands have been tied."

"I spent hours researching items to help consciousness. I can give you a dozen to put you to sleep but none offering the reverse. Anything I forge will be entirely experimental."

"For now, all we can do is to keep trying. Tao can meditate; the medics can tend to the unconscious; Kasim can return to the library and I'll consider what reinforcements might be most beneficial. Reconvene in an hour?"

"Agreed," multiple voices responded.

Sounds of people shuffling around continued, but the conversations had ended.

"I think I can help," Lena proposed.

"How so, little cub?"

"Sometimes I can see through things."

"Like x-ray vision?"

"No. Kohl called it 'True Sight' yesterday. Maybe I can see through the fog."

"I've never heard of that skill to know its risks. Plus, even if a break-in was possible, it's clearly dangerous down there. I don't think I could put you at risk like that, Lena."

"What if you helped? What if you gave me something that could connect us?"

"There is something I could do, but that carries even more risk." Solei's tone bordered on cynicism.

"I'm going to see if I can do this, Solei, with or without help."

Solei sighed. "Technology isn't the only conveyer of electricity. Neurons are too."

"Neurons? You can get into people's brains?"

"'Can' being the operative word. My talent is extremely controlled, except when I'm supercharged. Then anything, or anyone, close to me is fair game."

"Does it hurt the other person when you go into their mind?"

"If I do it poorly it will."

"Are you used to doing it well?"

"I avoid it profusely."

"How would we even get into Legacy?"

"I might know a way through the dorms and locker rooms. If we go to my place first, I could pick up an earpiece. That might help too."

"It's settled then. Earpiece. Stealth mode. Brain fusion."

"You are the worst linguist I've ever met. Too bad that having you go in unprotected sounds worse. I'll do it, but Lena I can't promise what I'll find if I go into your mind."

Lena felt uneasy at the thought. "I understand. I need to try this though. I need to find my place."

"To the dorms then!"

"To the dorms!"

~~~~~~~~~~~~~~~~~~~~~~~~~~~~~~

Lena was standing at the end of a dark tunnel. She had her earpiece secured. Solei had shown her the underground, overgrown passages leading from the dorms into the school grounds. They had no problem avoiding discovery on their way to the locker rooms. Their efforts all led to this—a tunnel leading into the training field where just beyond laid the day's calamity.

"I'm ready," Lena announced.

"I'm here," Solei said in support.

Lena made her way towards the fog. It smelled like fresh rain and sea salt. It was relaxing. Comforting. She closed her eyes to let the scent fill her soul. *This is what tranquility must feel like.*

A jolt burned her forehead from within. "That hurt!" Lena scowled.

"You stopped responding verbally and your synapse responses went way down. I didn't have a lot of options."

"Can we find a nicer wake-up call next time?"

"May I suggest staying conscious?"

"Fine."

"Can you see anything yet, Lena? If not, we should consider leaving."

"Not yet and wouldn't you be the first to know if I did? Hey! Wait! Shh."

She saw an outline of a blue hue in the distance. She got closer and crouched behind a pillar surrounding the courtyard. Kohl. What was he doing here? *Was he one of the special forces P.C. mentioned?* Lena studied his movements. He was silent, pacing, clearly terrified. A voice cried out from behind him.

"Come on. Stay with me. I didn't bring you here for you to fade out! You need to listen to me!"

There was another boy there. His silhouette was black, and as Lena crept along the mossy cobblestone towards the fountain, his shape only got darker. His hair glimmered in the fog, his pale skin blended into the misty background, and his eyes were deep black pits. The clothes he wore were tattered beyond repair.

"I can't hold this much longer. I don't want to abandon you, Delphine, but I'll be left with no choice soon."

While straining to get a better view, Lena fell into the fountain.

The boy started in alarm. His outline blazed with a fiery fury. "Who's there? No one should be there! I'll put you to sleep myself! I demand you show yourself at once!"

The fog vanished. The air became crystal clear. There he stood. Tall, muscular, a perfect combination of chiseled onyx and porcelain glass. The boy was completely engulfed in flames. Lena was stunned by his beauty.

"You!"

She sat upright in the fountain covered in a sticky substance.

"Your problem now." He shifted a heavy lump into her arms. She could hear people running towards her in the distance. She begged for answers from Solei, but Lena's earpiece had fallen out. She searched the water, but it was too murky to see through. This fluid was thicker than water. Lena waded through the dark, sticky, crimson wetness. She tried to stand. The lump almost slipped. She adjusted her hold only to find there was a bloody mermaid in her arms.

"LENA!" Her dad was running towards her. He was completely aghast, worse than he had ever been with her mom.

Lena was stupefied. She found herself standing in a fountain, covered in a bloody liquid, holding a mermaid. *This is probably not going to end well*, she opined as a familiar spark panged her forehead.

~~~~~~~~~~~~~~~~~~~~~~~~~~~

It had been a week. Her father had been silent for days. He never spoke about it, but there was an understanding that Lena was grounded for life. She attempted to plead her case a few times, but he simply held up his hand and walked away. She guessed her mom knew too. On Lena's second night at home, she heard her mother wailing and banging on the walls. Lena went to go help, but Kamilah's bedroom door stayed shut. It was clear she wasn't welcome.

Her friends texted on the first day of isolation, but then even they went silent. Airess had a million questions about who Lena saw in the mist. Solei had left a single message that they had to tell Airess everything, evidently due to some vague side effects. Based on the brief inquiries from Tao, Lena imagined he was also being asked a million questions by Airess. Of all her friends, he was the only one Lena could still get a response from. His messages were short and only happened if she asked him something directly, but they existed.

Lena hated being starved of communication, but answers that could shatter her heart were worse than silence. *Does anyone even miss me? Am I considered a random oddity now? Will I ever be allowed back?* Sometimes, in the night, she tried to use her True Sight. Lena hoped to find another blue outline out in the dark. If Kohl could cross into the fog, maybe he would appear near her too. Those moments seemed nothing more than pipe dreams.

Lena found herself completely alone, left with only her thoughts, for hours on end. One memory in particular replayed endlessly, the boy in flames. His outline was etched into her mind. The remembrance of him was hypnotizing. Even in reminiscence, they felt so brilliant and warm. Lena had no doubts his inferno could've burnt her to a crisp, yet it made her feel more alive than ever. She felt invigorated.

There was a knock at the door. She ran to open it. *Finally*. Her heart was racing. She threw the door open wide. No one was there. She peered around, nothing. As she retreated in dismay back to her room, she saw a note on her door:

"Leaving to talk to Principal Chromwell. Will let you know."

It wasn't a lot, but it was something. Lena ran to her phone.

She snapped a picture of the message, created a group chat, and hit send. Her body was almost vibrating in anticipation of what her friends' insights could be. There were so many questions to be asked.

"I hope it goes well, I'd hate to see you expelled so soon." The first message was from Tao. No surprise there.

Airess saw the message after that, then Solei, but neither responded. The infamous three dots appeared from Airess five or six times. That was as far as it went. Lena was crushed. The day passed. Her father hadn't come home; her mother remained quiet. Lena fed herself and went to bed early. As she was falling asleep, she saw a blue glow shrouded in twilight.

"Kohl?" She walked over half asleep. It was the glow of her phone, a text from an unknown number.

"Meet me in the fields behind the school ASAP! Be careful. Don't get caught!"

Without a second thought, Lena got ready and snuck out of her house. Off she went, recklessly, into the night.

Chapter 6
Secrets and Sirens

Lena ran the whole way to the agricultural fields. There were two silhouettes off to her right; she suspected they were Kohl and the boy from before. She stealthily snuck closer. She was about fifty feet away when a vine pulled her down to the ground; Lena covered her mouth to muffle her screams. Her phone fell from her coat pocket. A tendril twirled around the small rectangle; Lena stretched to grab it. The vine slithered away, retracting the phone deeper into the dense vegetation. Lena chased after it.

The phone traveled an easy path to the center of a sizable crop circle. Lena entered the small clearing and inspected the elevated platform in the middle. Herbs grew along the edges. The soil around the center smelled fresh. A green X was visible below Lena's phone. Recognizing she had been baited, she paused to focus on her surroundings. She couldn't sense any visual deceptions. Calmly, slowly, she strode to get her phone. A cloaked figure, brown as mud, emerged at the edge of the field. They were short in stature, barely more than a foot in height.

The platform Lena was on started to shake; she fell to her knees. The brown cloak rose and scouted the perimeter. Vines entwined around Lena, securing her in place but not constricting her. The plants worked rapidly, leaving a single gap for Lena to see through. As the figure grabbed a long pole from the dirt, two pink curls escaped outside their hood.

Airess started to mumble. Lena could feel herself moving again. She was being rolled across roots, dirt, and solid flooring. She broke twigs to make another peep hole. Light beamed in. The stark contrast irritated her eyes. She winced.

"Stop that! They'll see you!" Airess waved her hand over the hole. Darkness returned. A leaf popped into Lena's mouth; it tasted minty.

"Hi, checking in to see Ina." The movement ceased.

"Airess, I don't think it's your shift, pet."

"That's why I'm checking in. I read somewhere that peppermint could help stimulate a dormant mind. I've been working on this hybrid for months! I wanted to bring it to her while it was at peak potency!" Lena could hear Airess turn on her charm. She was impossible to resist.

"All right. You know the way. Don't stay too late. You're the first one on come tomorrow morning."

"I know! Thanks for always looking out for me, Nadea. Leaving soon?"

"I'll be out of your hair in a minute; I'm finishing up reports. You all take care. I'm trusting you."

The platform began moving once more, faster this time. Lena could hear Airess' indistinct mumbling again. Suddenly, Lena's lungs constricted.

"Airess ... air...." Lena gasped. The vines unraveled and made their way up onto the ceiling.

"Sorry! I forget others are so affected by the greenhouse's humidity. It feels like home to me." She helped her friend up. "How are you?"

"I'm fine." Lena responded dismissively. Airess skeptically raised her eyebrow. "Physically. Physically, I'm fine."

"Emotionally?" Airess held out her hands.

Lena's palms hovered over Airess'. "Promise me I can trust you?"

Airess concurred and Lena embraced her friend's power. The flood of emotions hit Airess unsuspectingly—loneliness, sadness, fear, anger, passion, determination. Airess was thrown from feeling to feeling like a rag doll, each equally powerful and vying for attention. Desperate for reprieve, Airess let go.

"I had no idea. We should talk." Airess grew two flowers for them to sit on.

"Let's start with where are we?" A mini forest outlined the structure of a room.

"This is Ina Jophiel's room. She's the reason I was brought to Astoria. I'm her primary caretaker in Ward A." Airess boasted slightly.

"Ward B you mean?"

"I meant Ward A. It used to be called The House of Ages."

"I don't know what that is. The only place I've seen with this much foliage is the Old Ha—" A palm leaf covered Lena's mouth.

"She can hear you!" Airess pointed over to a mound a few feet away. Lena eyed her friend then moved closer. An ornamented casket was adorned with flowers and leaves upon a draped catafalque. Ina was beautiful. Her hair matched the color of the earthen soil. Her skin was kissed by the sun. Clothes of silk draped over her, shimmering without reflecting any light. Resting below her were tufts of snow. No, Lena corrected, they were feathers crisp as snow arching from Ina's head to below her knees like wings.

"Airess ... is Ina ... is she an angel?"

"Close to it. She's a direct descendant of the angel Jophiel, hence the last name. Gods aren't very clever with human customs."

"This can't be who I think it is." Lena recalled all the imposed dread surrounding the notion of the Old Hag. "How can someone so beautiful receive such an awful title?"

"That, my friend, is a long story. One we don't have a lot of time for. Hold my hands and let me share a few things I've learned here at Legacy Academy."

~~~~~~~~~~~~~~~~~~~~~~~~~~~~~~

Lena was immobilized in astonishment. There was so much to take in.

"I really need your help. Please, Lena?" Airess' eyes brimmed with hope.

The Hall of Ages, it turns out, is a final resting place for gods. Not popular ones like Thor, more so for deities no one remembers. When societies stop believing in their gods, it causes the deities to lose their power. As their devoted worship fades away, so does their celestial being. Their descent from greatness opens a portal to Ward A. Previously, a team of elites called The Avenging Angels were sent in to retrieve these dissipating deities. The team's purpose was to bring the immortals to Ward A, where their diminished forms would be cared for eternally.

Evidently, there were two major complications within this process. First, as time went on, more and more gods were being forgotten. Many religions became mythologies. Entire verbal traditions were obliterated. Secondly, the last member of the elite team, T.A.A, was Ina Jophiel. Airess phrased her status as "no longer active." However, since Lena could see an unconscious body in a casket, she interpreted the situation to be slightly graver than Airess let on.

Those weren't the only imperative facts either. Airess was also able to share insights into what the "blood" in the fountain ended up being, that her healing abilities extended to any living organism, and, most importantly, that the boy Lena could not get out of her mind had a name. Diablo. He was named after the devil. That was a surprise, to say the least.

"Are you sure that's not another misleading nickname?" Lena's heart was in conflict.

"Siren? No, I'm pretty sure that's how they identify." Airess appeared confused.

Oh, right. Her focus was on saving the siren—not mermaid— that appeared in the fountain. Lena vaguely remembered Airess suggesting a godly rescue mission. Also, maybe something about restoring the T.A.A. or maybe it was about rebranding?

"Lena, we only have a few hours left and these missions take a lot of time. Plus, we don't have permission, so we have to go unnoticed. Principal Chromwell would go mad if she knew about this!" Airess paused thinking of all the horrible outcomes. "Will you please go with me? I don't think I can do this alone."

Lena was never great at turning down a friend in need. "Okay. Count me in."

"YAY!" Airess cheered and tackled Lena with a hug. "Our first team mission!"

Airess quickly explained the technical rules they needed to adhere to and how they would be breaking all of them. *Airess the rebel, who knew?* She explained that once they entered the portal, they'd become a part of that world.

In this case, they'd likely become something seaworthy. Airess made sure to explain that there was no control over what part of the realm they'd become. Lena prayed she'd be something more useful than a clump of seaweed.

The mission sounded simple enough—go into the portal, find the deity, bring them back to Ward A, be praised as life savers, done. The mist escapade was way more complex and dangerous. Airess rushed to grab vests and a few items from around the room. Once she had stuffed every pocket they had with herbs and oddities, she led them down the winding halls to the portal.

The portal had energy to it. Lena could feel it before she saw it. She wished Solei was there. The scent of saltwater filled the air. As Lena and Airess rounded the corner, the portal was impossible to miss. It was a half-moon outlined in wet coral and squashy moss. The ingress looked like a stormy whirlpool. This mission suddenly felt less inviting.

"On three?" Airess, as always, held out her hand.

"On three." Lena held on tight, preparing to spring into the eye of a hurricane, literally.

"One, two, three!" The girls vaulted forward.

The water was cold and harsh. The centrifugal force kept them swirling. The individual waves pulled, tossed, and rolled them. The water crashed from side to side. Lena was too scared to breathe, too scared to open her eyes. Her only focus was to hold on to Airess' hand for dear life. The common factor, amidst all the external chaos, was the pressure pulling them deeper. Not one movement ever went upwards. Terror started to creep into Lena's mind. *What if we drown?* The water above only got heavier. Light only became scarcer. Her grip on Airess strained. Lena could feel kicks near her face. *She's swimming.* Lena started to kick too. She swam straight into a rock.

"Open your eyes, Lena!" Airess' voice sounded distorted. It reminded Lena of yelling underwater at the local pool as a child.

A large log came shooting Lena's way. She moved to dodge it and closed the gap between her and her friend. Airess indicated a cavern not so far away. Lena bobbed in acknowledgement. They had to push through the current to reach it. Their task was strenuous, but the bond of their hands magnified the determination of the two girls. They had only been in this world for a few minutes and Lena's body was already getting sore.

Airess pointed up towards an air pocket, and Lena followed. "We can breathe underwater, but I thought this might help you adapt. We're all right down here, but I need more from you."

Lena knew Airess was right. It felt so disorienting though. She did not have natural mermaid instincts. Which reminded Lena, she checked her lower body.

"We have feet!" Lena announced, slightly perplexed.

Airess giggled. "Yes, Lena. We're human. We have feet."

"But I thought we would adapt to our surroundings. We have no fins, no gills, and no tails. We're so boring," Lena groaned.

"I say this with love, Lena, but you need to stop thinking about yourself. We're in the midst of a god's final moments. This needs to be about them. Deities are the epitome of entitlement. If we want to convince them to come back with us, we have to fuel their ego. Their entire existence has been completely based on humans worshiping them." Airess judged Lena's demeanor. "If we are truly humans here, our best scenario is getting this deity to see us as personal servants."

"And the worst scenario?" Lena prodded.

"They eat us."

"Eat us?!"

Airess shrugged. "It could happen. All I know is that the siren you found in the fountain is fading away. That same day, this sea-based portal appeared in Ward A. I strongly believe if we save this deity, we can save both."

Lena was barely paying attention the first time Airess explained the situation, but in her head the speech sounded a lot more absolute.

"We're the best chance they have. Can you keep your eyes open? Gods enjoy playing games with mortals. Deceptions are practically guaranteed."

Next time, I need to pay attention better. "On it. I'm ready."

Airess plunged straight down from the cavern's ledge, staying along the outside of the spinning funnel. Lena focused on anything that seemed to move irregularly. The vortex of the whirlpool carried a lot of debris but nothing jarring. As the pair continued their path, the edges around them transformed from water to rock. Narrow passageways were beginning to form. Lena and Airess were swimming past the ocean floor, deeper into the earth.

A blue speck glinted off the last ray of light. Lena pulled Airess back; her arm jabbed into a jagged edge. A thin stream of blood spiraled by. Airess' eyes became wide and both her hands immediately surrounded the wound. She worked with absolute concentration. Lena tried to spot the blue light again. The abyss before them was pitch black. A rumble shook from below.

Lena sought direction from her friend, but Airess was too engulfed in her work. The vibrations were getting stronger. A guttural roar paired with the shaking. Lena wrapped Airess with her wounded arm and started towards the previous light. She had no idea where to go, but without being able to see, she knew they stood no chance. Rocks started to fall from above. The vibrations were causing a rockslide. Lena attempted to navigate past the wreckage to get to open water. The noise grew as did the strength of the center funnel. Lena was no match for its power.

Airess shrieked as the pair fell victim to the maelstrom. The shrillness pierced Lena's ears. She lost track of her surroundings. She barely detected the colossal boulder descending upon them. With no time to spare, she braced for the hit. Pain extended through her entire body. Her head slammed against the rock. An immense boom resounded. Lena let go of her composure and started to cry. This entire plan was too much.

"Shh. I need you to be quiet right now. We need to wait until the guardian passes." The voice wasn't Airess'. It was a male voice. Lena searched for her friend; cold

stone was all she could find. *Airess!*
Lena muffled her cries, but her
heart ached.

He held her close and the
world calmed. "There, I think it's
gone now. I can probably move this
rock, but I could use some help.
What's your role here?" Lena didn't
answer. "Do you have any powers?"
Lena's voice was stifled. He was
getting frustrated. "First you and
your friend glide on in here like it's
nothing, you make one dumb
decision after the next, get yourself
cut enough to draw the serpent out
for blood, and now you can't, or
won't, speak? Fantastic. This is why
only trained angels were allowed in
these portals. I'm glad you're mute."
He punched the wall. "Let me see

your arm. I want to see if Airess finished the healing process." *He knew Airess.* Lena gave him her arm. His touch was warm. A sense of comfort washed over her. *It couldn't be him, could it?* "At least she did something right." He took hold of Lena's chin. "Can you speak?"

Lena met his gaze. His eyes blazed like the sun. *It was him.* "Yes."

"What powers did you keep here?" He spoke steadily and deliberately.

"I can see." *I can see you.* "I mean I can see through illusions and some other stuff, I think."

"That has nothing to do with Hera, Sirens, or Muses. What talents did you get from this world?"

Hera? "That's all I know."

"Terrific." He had no intention of hiding his anger. "Based on that nasty shriek your friend let out, I'm guessing she's a siren down here. That wouldn't help move this boulder, but maybe we can shatter it. I'll push. You try to scream as loud as you can. Deal?"

Lena braced herself, filled her heart with all of the frustrations and pain she'd felt since the move, and let it out in one echoing screech. Not only did the stone shatter, but the explosion was controlled with her voice. Increasing her pitch, Lena sent the fragments upwards, aiming to clear an opening. This new power was strong. Lena flopped against the wall and slid down.

"That ... that is one way to handle a situation." Diablo watched the debris soar. "The guardian hasn't come back yet and the music stopped. That means the whirlpool will have dissipated too."

"That's a good thing, right?" Lena asked optimistically.

"It could be. It could also mean our god's dead. There's only one way to find out." He dove off the edge.

Lena was so tired. She swore she could feel agony in every cell in her body. She had never felt so depleted in all her life. She couldn't fight the urge to rest.

"Normally, when two people are in a dangerous situation together and one leaves, the other sticks close behind. If you don't, that ruins the whole dynamic and, instead, I come off like a jerk who's abandoned you." He nudged her with his foot. Lena smacked him away. "You know we're in water; floating would be significantly less dramatic."

"Go. I'll catch up with you. I need a couple minutes."

"This is why training your abilities is paramount. I bet you overexerted yourself with that wail. I can't leave you here. That guardian will be back sooner or later and they're already chasing your scent. I can't believe I'm doing this, but climb on." He was kneeling in front of Lena impatiently.

"Seriously?"

"I'm almost guaranteed to change my mind. Make it quick."

Lena wrapped her arms around his neck, her legs around his waist, and nuzzled in. Her eyes stayed closed as they swam. She could feel the waves on her skin and his hair tickling her face.

"I can see Airess at the bottom. Hopefully she's better at persuasion than she was at taking care of you."

"I'm fine," Lena protested.

"Then can you detach yourself?"

"I'm also comfy. Onward stead!" She clicked her heels into him.

"You are the worst person I've ever met. I would drop you if it wouldn't make me responsible for killing you." There was playfulness in his complaints.

"What's your name?"

"Diablo."

"No, I don't believe that. What's your real name?"

"Have you attended Legacy at all? Don't they teach you that gods don't give their real names out unless tricked?"

"So, you're a god?"

"No, I'm an angel. Which is why I belong in this portal and you do not."

"You're really an angel?" Lena remarked in wonderment.

"I'm Diablo, the devil! Lucifer? Don't you know anything?" His body was heating up as his anger rose; it was like hugging a heated blanket.

"This is only my third time on campus."

He stopped. "Please tell me Miss Goody Two Shoes down there did not bring you through a portal when you've only known your powers for three days?"

Lena pondered his assertion. "It's been a week since the fountain, right? I think that makes it eight?"

"The school has been shut down this whole week! Have you even had a full week of classes?"

"I've yet to make it through a day. Things have been difficult lately." Lena floated over his head to look into his intense eyes. She couldn't read his emotions.

Diablo stared at her. "I apologize in advance, but if your friend is not dead by the time we find her, I may kill her." He left and dropped to the realm's floor.

"Come back here!" Lena chased after him.

He hadn't gone far before hiding behind a barrier. His eyes switched to solid black. Lena maintained her distance and surveyed the area for information. She saw an outline of Kohl. He was arguing. Lena treaded closer. He was arguing with Airess.

"For the last time, where did he take her, Kohl? Where did that demon take Lena?"

"For the last time, Airess, I. Don't. Know! Bringing her here was a huge mistake. You've got to see that now. Lena has no place here, she barely belongs in Legacy. You're just mad because it's your fault if she dies."

"I care because she's my friend!"

"We're friends too, or did you forget? You couldn't save me, so now you need to try to save her?"

"It's not like that, Kohl, and we are still friends."

"Funny. It sure doesn't seem that way. You stopped asking me for help in Ward A almost immediately after you found out what I was."

"Your lineage has nothing to do with this, but I have to admit that associating with the devil doesn't help your cause."

"Diablo happened after us and you know it." A blue hue reached for Airess' face. Lena watched her swipe it away.

"My biggest mistake was thinking there was an 'us' to begin with. Alive, dead, undead. None of it matters if you can't face who you are. Are you going to help me find her or not, Kohl?"

"Nope. Not this time, Airess. You're going to have to save yourself for once. I'm getting out of here. Time's almost up and I'm not staying trapped for eternity with a ravenous sea beast and a featherless bird woman. Good luck." Kohl dematerialized.

Lena couldn't stand to listen to any more. Since she had entered Legacy, she'd always felt like a pawn in someone else's game. She was determined to live by her own rules. She recognized a large shell off in the distance. *The deity*. Lena decided to end this.

The pit was void of all light, but the inside of the conch shell acted like a stark white lantern. The goddess lay peacefully asleep on top of a giant harp. Her hair was made of sparse golden threads that matched the strings of the instrument. Her torso was as delicate as powder. Her legs were scaled and opalescent.

"Hello?" Lena tried to jostle the goddess. "I'm Lena. I'd like to take you somewhere safe." Nothing happened. "Please." She stood by for a response. When none came, she crawled into the shell to lift the body. If the deity could not go to Ward A of her own accord, Lena would shoulder the weight herself. A harp string caught on her nail.

A familiar roar sounded in the distance—the guardian.

"Lena! Stop! You don't understand!" Voices called from behind, voices that she knew didn't believe in her.

Standing on the harp, Lena continued to maneuver the sea goddess. The instrument played off her steps. Lena's toes slid and plucked the strings as she steadied to balance the deity in her arms. The goddess was shockingly sturdy. Her body didn't fall apart like powder in the slightest. Lena wrapped her in the surrounding cloth and darted straight up.

A growl rang out in the small space. The beast was close. Lena could see stark white feathers outlining the opening. She set her sight on them, ignoring all else. Attached to those feathers, unfortunately, was a snake with the head of a bird. Its beak spread wide, exposing thousands of fangs dripping discolored venom. Lena had accidentally aimed herself right down the middle. Its bill jutted across the entire opening. The guardian lunged towards her.

"GO!" A blue light hurtled in front of her. The serpent's jaws snapped closed, missing Lena by centimeters.

Screams increased below. Lena kept swimming. Past the cave she shared with Diablo. Past the opening of the chasm. Past the cavern Airess first brought her to. Past the water, into the air. Lena's blindness returned but by light instead of darkness. She never stopped. Lena stayed moving until she could feel no more. There was a pop, like a bubble. A small splash. Gravity hit heavy. *Air.*

Lena inhaled a deep breath. *Ward A.* She wrapped the sleeping goddess in the extra clothes Airess had given her. Unused herbs and items spilled from the pockets, a mess of spoiled, good intentions.

Perhaps Kohl was right, Diablo too. Maybe none of this was for her. It wouldn't be the first time Lena had found herself unable to fit in.

Using exit signs to guide her way, it didn't take long for her to find her escape.

"Don't forget to sign out!" a receptionist called from behind a desk. Lena played along.

"Sure. Sorry." She traced over the last name written there. Diablo. Diablo was the last seventeen names written on this page. He was the sole visitor in the last ten months. "Thanks." Lena passed back the pen and departed. The door opened into Ward B, right by the bed of the man who had heckled Ms. Galen. This was the door Airess freaked out about the other day.

Lena made her way across the infirmary, casually glancing at the patient beds. She was curious to see the siren and reap any sights of a job well done. A groan came from a few beds down. Lena peeked in. Solei. They were caked in mud. Their face was contorted in pain. *What happened?*

Alarms began to beep. They sounded from behind. Lena peered over. The siren. Lena needed to leave. She bolted out of the building. She pushed on until she reached the street outside the school. Her lungs were hurting now too.

"Airess, when you said to meet you here at midnight, I didn't think you'd look like a swamp creature," commented Tao. "Oh man, or smell like one! What did you do, Airess?" Lena met his eyes. "Oh. Hi, Lena."

"Tao, Airess probably orchestrated you to be my ride. Not giving everyone the full story is her speciality."

"Ouch. Whatever you two did must not have gone well." He opened the door for her.

"I don't know. I never get to know anything." She got in.

"Sorry for whatever happened, Lena."

"It's not your fault."

"Actually, I wouldn't be so sure of that, Lena." He sighed.

"Why? What did you do, Tao?"

"I used my gift; then I told people about it." His tone carried so much regret. "I've been in almost nonstop meditation to help P.C. because of the mist and the only premonition I've received was about you."

"Doesn't she have teachers for that? Why was it about me?"

"They help too, but I'm her apprentice. Just like Airess is Ms. Galen's. We get some special treatment when it's time to use our abilities. Our bonds with them can help amplify either side's powers. As for why you, I don't know. I've asked myself that a lot too."

"You sure have a way with words, Tao. What did it tell you?"

The car parked in front of Lena's house. "I saw Principal Chromwell handing your dad transfer papers." There was an awkward silence.

"How often are your visions misconstrued? I've always heard prophecies are intentionally misleading. Are yours like that?"

"Prophecies are barely premonitions. I wish I could tell you mine were so vague."

"I'm disappointed but not surprised." Lena said her goodbyes and went into her house. It was dark; her parents had already fallen asleep. She climbed right into her bed. That night, Lena didn't even attempt her True Sight before she closed her eyes. There was no point now. No one wanted her in Astoria. The night had been too eventful and she was done.

Chapter 7
Transfers and Training

There was a knock on Lena's door. "Hey Magpie, you awake?"

Lena rolled over to face her dad. "Mostly. I'm not feeling like getting out of bed today."

Kasim sat next to his daughter. "I can't imagine everything you're going through right now. I know I'm still recovering from the image of you in that fountain and that's probably only a tenth of what's recently happened."

"It's sure been a lot. I won't deny that."

"When I met with Principal Chromwell yesterday, I did some self-reflection too. I think I let you down. I thought you could ease into all the godly stuff at Legacy Academy. I forgot how savage high school can be. Your mom and I, we never really had to experience all this."

"You never experienced high school? You two always said you were high school sweethearts."

Kasim sighed. "We did; we were. Things were just different back then."

"I feel like that's a cliché excuse."

"It is and yet still true. Your mom and I met at Legacy, but it was also the first real school I ever attended." He watched his daughter's face turn to shock. "You probably didn't know that, huh? You have to be tired of so many surprises. Why don't we go downstairs? I'll brew some tea and answer every question you can conjure up." Her dad patted Lena's bed and rose.

"Dad, before we go downstairs, I need to know one thing."

"Anything. Shoot."

"Am I going back to my classes when school reopens?"

Kasim stammered over his words. His internal struggle was apparent.

"Dad?" Lena could feel her last bits of hope fading away.

"I tried, Lena. Theodora's argument was incredibly persuasive. I couldn't refute. It's not all bad though! Your new training will be more tailored to you specifically. You won't have to try to act like everyone else. You can be you." He handed her a stack of folded papers from his back pocket. She threw them across the room. Tao was right.

"I'll be downstairs when you're ready. I've set aside the whole day. I love you, Magpie."

Lena turned away, and when she heard her door close, she wept. She felt like a failure. A failure to her friends. A failure to her dad. A failure to herself. It felt like no matter what she did, it wasn't enough. She criticized herself for not being able to make it through a full day of classes. *No wonder the mist and the portal went so poorly. What was I thinking? Being here doesn't make me special.* Relying on those around her to tell her who she was wasn't working and letting them decide her fate, or her worth, had turned out even worse.

Lena recalled the screams she'd heard after Kohl saved her from the jaws of that awful guardian. *Poor Kohl.* Solei had already been hospitalized because of Lena. Who else would meet a similar fate, or worse? She couldn't imagine it. If she wanted to keep helping her friends, assuming she still had friends left to help, she needed to get better. She needed to commit to her own beliefs. Diablo's words echoed in her mind. Lena needed to be trained. Despite all her internal lashings, she knew she was smart. She knew she was fast. Those qualities were a solid starting point. It was time to be responsible and take control of her life. No more helplessness.

With a reformed sense of stubbornness and determination, she got ready to head downstairs. The aroma from the kitchen was tantalizing. Cinnamon and rose water filled the air, sahlab. It was her absolute favorite Egyptian delicacy. Sahlab tasted like a warm hug.

"Hey! You came down quick. I planned on making tea but thought this might be even better!" He looked so happy seeing his plan succeed.

Lena sat down at the counter and began picking at the plate of crushed pistachios. They were toppings for the drink, but she would always eat too many of them ahead of time. When she was a toddler, she would sneak away with them and come back for more. A decade later, there was comfort in exposing her gluttony. Kasim grinned at his daughter as he served them both.

"Dad, I don't want to leave Astoria." Lena kept her eyes focused on her mug.

"Me neither, Lena. We need to make some changes though. If you'll let me, I'd like to start training you. I won't lie, I'll need to request help from my colleagues when we get to the advanced lessons, but I can surely handle the basics."

"Colleagues?" Lena never remembered her father working with anyone before.

"Yes, that was part of the deal to keep you here in Astoria. I'm the newest guest lecturer at the academy."

"You're going to work at the same school that just kicked me out?" Her voice cracked.

"I can see how you'd feel that way. To me, joining their team was the best of both worlds. I'll be at the school often enough to keep tabs on what's going on in the main building and after some training, predominantly about safety, you can start your new lessons in Ward A and keep tabs on the gods."

"Wait. What?" *Ward A? Seriously?*

"Didn't I hand you the papers? You're being transferred from campus to a work program, essentially. You'll still have the potential to earn credits and graduate with your friends.

Theodora ... err Principal Chromwell ... is incredibly passionate about it. It seems you have a knack for being in places you shouldn't be. Instead of hindering your instincts, she wants you to master them."

Lena had those same ideas not even an hour before. The similarity was unsettling. "How did she know?"

"I'm not sure what you're referring to, but knowing and seeing all tends to be her speciality. Theodora had astonishing talents in school, but I'd like to believe my staff plays a sizable role now too."

"Your modesty becomes you," Lena teased, throwing a pistachio chunk at him.

"Hey! I'm allowed to be proud. I had to keep that eye in formaldehyde for months. My workshop reeked. My nose will never smell the same again!"

"Look at you all worked up. Also, the idea of an eyeball on her staff is disgusting. Eww."

"Theodora always called it Odin's eye. I intentionally never asked any questions."

Lena gagged. "Gross. I didn't know you all were so close."

Kasim grabbed a picture from the mantle. "We all were. Theodora, Ina, Averi, your mom, and I." They all had their arms around one another, laughing. Her mom looked so happy. So normal. Lena's finger lingered over her. Kasim cut in. "She was brilliant, you know? Smart as anyone, clever too. No one could out-strategize your mom. Kamilah, my Millie, was the best." Kasim's voice was getting choked up. "Not that she isn't now. I didn't mean...."

Lena consoled her dad. "I can't imagine a change like that."

"She had no business being with a boy like me. I was an orphaned kid plucked from the desert, thrown into a life opposite my own, and Millie was basically Legacy royalty. There wasn't a single person who didn't know who she was or who she was related to. She was beautiful, beyond intelligent, overly generous, and had a pedigree that rivaled that of European monarchs. To know Millie was to love Millie. She commanded every room she walked into and we all fell to her feet."

How is that the same person who once smashed every plate in the kitchen because she couldn't find a saucer for her coffee? "What happened?" Tears were welling for Lena too. She lost her mom before she ever had her. Life could have been so different.

Kasim put the photo back. "We were kids rescuing gods." *Omg ... they were The Avenging Angels.* "We thought we were invincible. Turns out, gods are invincible. Kids, less so. A mission went sour, people panicked, bad calls were made. A goddess got mad and took what Millie cherished most. Your mom lost her mind in a very literal sense. The whole group fell apart after that. Ina blamed herself; Averi left Ward A. Theodora tried to act like everything was the same, but Millie needed help. I couldn't find what we needed here, so we left. I had no idea what she needed, but I wasn't going to stop searching until she regained peace of mind."

"But you never did. You never found a cure for her."

"Lena, your mom may get confused often, but she's found balance within herself. She found her purpose again."

Those were optimistic words about someone who could barely

231

perform basic domestic functions. Lena shrugged her shoulders.

"Every obscure pairing of socks, unique room rearrangement, or new painting experiment, they're all acts of kindness towards her family. She wants us to be as eager to come home to her as she is to us. Your mom may not always be able to comprehend her surroundings, but her love for us is impenetrable."

Lena recounted all the times she had secretly wished her mom was anyone else, especially at the peaks of her cognitive disruptions. Lena promised herself that, next time, she'd be more understanding. She'd do her best to meet her mom with love instead of frustration amidst the chaos.

"Is Mom an angel?"

"No, why do you ask?"

"I heard in order to go through the portals you had to be an angel."

Kasim chuckled. "Time has a way of distorting information and Legacy has a way of making up tall tales. No. I hate to disappoint, but neither of us are angels. The Egyptian god Ptah is my patron, and despite your mother's ancestors believing they're descendants of the god Allah, the angel Jibril chose to be your mom's patron."

Allah? Allah was the central god to the entire Islamic religion. She remembered her mom scoffing about Zeus the night of the sock mishap. *No kidding*, Lena thought.

Who needs Grandpa to be in a trio of kings when he can be the entire top of the pyramid? "That's huge! Why didn't you say anything?"

"We don't really believe it to be true and it isn't a part of our lives anymore, Lena. A lot of lineages can be highly speculative. There isn't proof to make them factual. Some people start declaring, 'Hey, we're this!' and if they're convincing enough, then the label sticks."

Lena thought back to Tao's similar views about the Oracles. "I feel like if I said I was a descendant of Allah, people would laugh in my face."

"I've heard of some struggles you've had there. Wanna talk about it, Magpie? I'm also a little surprised you've heard about Ward A. After Millie got hurt and then poor Ina, I was under the impression the house was off limits."

"That's not an inaccurate interpretation of facts." Lena's pulse started to race. Time to come clean.

"More sahlab then?" Kasim reached for her cup.

"And cookies? On the couch? This might take a while."

~~~~~~~~~~~~~~~~~~~~~~~~~~~~

"Try again, Lena. If you're going to let your life hang on the actions of a fallen angel, I need you to concentrate." Kasim blew a cloud out of a whistle and lifted his daughter back to the top of the canyon.

"Very funny, Dad." Lena was breathy as she leaped from obstacle to obstacle.

Kasim had taken the news of Lena's adventures better than she anticipated. His biggest upset, which she should have seen coming, was her being alone with boys unsupervised. The tiny cave with Diablo took a lot more explanation, and reassurance, than running into the mist with Solei melded into her mind. Shortly after her dad calmed down, he had asked Lena to join him in his workshop. He picked out a carpet and unrolled it for them; the tapestry created an actual gorge they could travel to. Lena had been practicing jumping, and falling, ever since.

"Bend your knees! Keep your center of balance low! You're exposing yourself, you'll get knocked over!" Another blow of the whistle; a gust of wind knocked her off the ledge. Another plump cloud was ready to retrieve her. This time, Lena was delivered right to her dad.

"I've got this. I can go again." She got up and dusted herself off.

"I need to go check in on your mom." With a wave of his hand they were back in the woodshop, the rug curled by their feet. "Take these for the night. They're like virtual reality glasses. Think of the scene you want and they'll take you there."

"How close to reality are they? Will it hurt when I fall?"

A look of concern passed over Kasim. "I recommend not falling." He patted her on the head. "Good luck, Magpie! I'll be around if you need me."

Lena took the items to her bedroom. She hopped in the shower and then went back downstairs. It had been a while since she cooked for her family and tonight seemed perfect. Her mom and dad were watching the television together. Kamilah was flipping from one channel to the next every couple of seconds. When dinner was done, Lena delivered the plates to the living room.

"Do I smell coconut rice? That's my favorite!" Her mom was elated.

"I remembered. Coconut rice and jerk chicken." Lena rubbed her mom's shoulder.

"Thank you!" Kamilah continued smelling her dish.

"I agree, thank you, Magdelena." Her dad turned off the TV while they ate together.

"I heard you both in the shop today. What were you doing?" her mom asked with her mouth full.

"I was training Lena. We were working on her balance."

"Dad was knocking me off a cliff with a whistle," Lena playfully jabbed.

"At least you weren't underwater. Wind gusts are horrible there. They hit you in the stomach once and you're useless for a solid few minutes." Kamilah spoke tactfully.

Lena couldn't recall the last time the three of them had enjoyed an actual conversation. Kasim looked surprised too. His wife never talked of their previous excursions.

"What do you recommend for Lena, sweetheart?" Kasim was testing the boundaries of Kamilah's cognisance.

"Weighted shoes. Wait, no. That'll make it harder to jump. I know! Tomorrow, I can tie weights to your left shoe and balloons to your right shoe!"

Lena smiled. "It certainly can't make me much worse. Why not?"

Kamilah was beaming with happiness. They finished their dinner and Lena went to sit on the floor. She leaned against the couch her parents were on. Her mother reached down to play with her hair. Lena relaxed, soaking in the moment. Taking time to appreciate those closest to her was the best practice Lena had done all day.

"I hate to break up our evening, but we need our rest. Big days are ahead of us." Kasim stood and held out his hands to his wife and daughter.

"I love you guys." Lena pulled them into a family hug.

"I'm not a guy, but I love you too," her mom corrected.

They all got ready for bed. Once Lena was settled in, she inspected the glasses. They were tempting. Not to envision cliffs and ravines but to picture herself with her friends. She longed to have a photo like her dad had. Lena, Solei, Tao, possibly Airess, or even Kohl, and of course Diablo, all wrapped up in one quintessential snapshot she could hold on to forever.

~~~~~~~~~~~~~~~~~~~~~~~~~~~

Lena woke up to her alarm. There was paper covering the snooze button.

"Urgent matter at Legacy. I'll hurry back soon.

Practice while I'm gone. Love, Dad."

She reached for her phone. Sure enough, there were texts awaiting her.

The first one she opened was from Tao. "Hey, do you mind if I talk to Airess about some of the things you mentioned in the car last night?" The text was almost a day old. Another followed. "Waiting isn't my best quality. I talked to Airess. I'm not saying I agree with you, but she would not talk about the other night at all. I hate to admit it, but I think she might be hiding something too."

Speaking of the healer, she had also sent a single message. "Lena! I need to talk to you!" Airess had called ten times the day before.

Lena would call her soon, but she wasn't ready yet. She texted Tao. "Hey, I just got to my phone." She was working on a follow-up message when he replied.

"Did Airess reach out to you? She promised she'd call you herself. Things are bad, Lena, things are really bad."

Anxiety hit like a ton of bricks. *Oh no.* "She did. I missed her message and all her calls. What happened?!"

"It's Kohl. He's not waking up. I can't get any information out of Airess. He's been unconscious since the other night."

NO! Lena had to see him. She was filling her backpack when her mom knocked on the door.

"Good morning! I'm here for your shoes." Kamilah saw her daughter in tears. "Magdalena, what's wrong?"

"It's all my fault, Mom. My friend tried to save me and he got really hurt. I'm sure he's in Ward B. I'm headed there now."

"Theodora said no. Kasim told me. He was so distraught over it. You're not allowed anymore."

Lena was trying to hold herself together, but she was losing her grip. "Mom, I have to go. Two friends are hospitalized from helping me. I need to hold myself accountable for this."

"Stay here, please. One moment." Kamilah hurried to her room and back. "Take my blanket with you."

"Mom, that's really sweet, but—" Her mom draped the blanket over Lena's arm. It disappeared. The blanket was magic.

"I ... I'd like it back. It's very important to me."

Confused, Lena offered it back to her mom.

"Not now, after. I need it for when my mind turns on me. It helps protect me; it's kept me safe for years. Today, I want that for you. You need it."

The blanket must have been how her dad always calmed her mom. At her mom's worst moments, she got to do what everyone dreamed of—Kamilah could become invisible to the outside world. *What a selfless gift.*

Lena hugged the blanket. "Thank you. I'll take special care of it. I promise."

"I believe you. Now go before we get caught." Kamilah winked.

Lena gave her mom the biggest hug and ran out the door.

Ward B was more than a mile away, but she made good time. She stared at the building evaluating the best way to sneak in. There was a glimmer outlining the structure.

Lena concentrated. The glimmer was shaped like another building, but it was so expansive she could only see the front. The shape took over the area but on another plane of existence. *Ward A.* Lena walked along the side of Ward B. There was a door, but it was locked. She peeped through a nearby window. Airess was tending to a patient. *Yes!*

Lena tapped on the glass trying to get Airess' attention, but it wasn't working. Emotions, Airess always talked about how sensitive she was to them. Lena began screaming her friend's name in her mind while she tapped. *Airess!*

The head of bubble gum hair spun around immediately. Lena waved. Airess hurried to the door.

"What are you doing here? Why didn't you just answer my phone calls?"

"I didn't have my phone. Let me in. What happened to Kohl?"

"I can't, Lena. I'm not on the staff's good side right now and I know you're not a student at Legacy anymore."

"Isn't this the community hospital too? Trust me. I have a plan." Lena wished Airess had Solei's talents, but reassurance and goodwill were going to have to suffice. She took her friend's hand.

"Ugh. Okay, but this had better be good. They'll have our heads if we cause any more trouble."

Lena hoped that was a figure of speech. Regardless, she wrapped herself up in the blanket and snuck in. The surprise on Airess' face was already worth it. Lena found Kohl's bed; it was next to Solei's. There was a chair in between them.

Pretending to do rounds, Airess grabbed Kohl's chart and quietly started reading. "Patient admitted November 4th, 2:00 a.m. Found unresponsive. Insurmountable, small puncture wounds. Four larger puncture wounds found on their torso. Source remains unknown. All wounds seeping fizzing murkish liquid. Classification unknown.

Vitals stable. Blood tests sent to lab November 4th 10:07 p.m."

Lena couldn't make eye contact. When he had saved her, he'd ended up completely engulfed by the guardian. Whatever venom the creature produced now pumped through Kohl's veins too.

A beep came from the other side of Lena. It was Solei. Their heart rate monitor was rapidly increasing.

"Oh no, not again," a voice across the aisle whined. Lena recognized her from the fountain.

Airess pushed a button on the monitors that issued an alarm within the building. "Mud! I need mud and space to work!" She clicked a setting on the large blanket over Solei; it began to hum. The lights started to flicker above. "Now please! I need those bandages now!"

Staff started to fill the room, led by Ms. Galen. They were all carrying large buckets filled with a brown sloshing substance. Lena pushed the chair out of the way and relocated herself, giving Airess space to cover their friend in muddy bandages.

Solei looked radiant. Glowing, even. The room's temperature was drastically increasing as well. Tiny little sparks danced over their skin. They were starting to move. Their face contorted and they gave a loud wail.

"Shh. Shh. I've got you. We've got this. You just need to take some deep breaths." Another cry of pain. Solei thrashed their arm, sending bandages flying across the room. "No, no, no, no, no. Come on, try to relax." Airess had one hand over Solei's forehead and the other on their heart. Ms. Galen was across the bed from her protégé, eyes closed, holding on to Airess' shoulders. The two healers had a special energy about them.

A zap sprung from Solei's foot and crashed into the wall. The siren shrieked, sending anyone conscious to their knees in pain. Airess remained steady and unfazed, chanting softly to Solei. Lena felt slightly jealous. She wanted to be that strong and composed. The monitor stopped beeping. The air became less humid. The room exhaled.

"I'm proud. You did well, Airess." Ms. Galen was trying to console her visibly upset student.

Airess shook her head. "This isn't sustainable. Solei can't keep enduring this." She pushed past the crowd of aides. "I need a minute." Into Ward A she went; Lena trailed close behind. Airess went straight to Ina's room. When Lena closed the door behind them, Airess draped her in a hug.

"I'm so sorry. I'm trying so hard to save them. I really am, Lena. I can feel your change of feelings towards me, but I swear on everything that I'm doing all I can for Solei. I'm just running out of straws to grab. It's like treating an exploding star. You try to prevent the supernova, but you know they're destined to burn up and explode. Solei doesn't even want me to save them. They want to deplete their energy. I don't know what else to do."

"That's a lot to put on yourself. You're not even fully trained, are you? Whatever happens, you've gone above and beyond for Solei. I've seen it. You were so impressive. Your best is all you can offer and that needs to be enough."

"I guess." Airess walked over and put her hand on Ina's

encasement. "I can't save her either."

"That's not your job, Airess. You're supposed to care for the ill, not be each one's savior."

"Now you sound like Kohl."

"I heard an argument you two had the last night we were all together. It sounded pretty heated."

"We function well enough in a group setting, but one-on-one we struggle. He was the first person I tried to save and couldn't at Legacy."

"Seems like a pattern, and from what I overheard, I'm your next damsel to fail at saving?"

Airess cringed. "When you say it like that, it doesn't sound as altruistic as it does in my head."

"You are amazing at what you do and I promise we will all take advantage of your healing abilities in due time, but you know what we need the most?"

"Not a clue."

"A good friend. One that we can trust, and talk to, and rely on. I know I definitely need that. When I thought you used me, losing our relationship hurt worse than any physical action."

"I never meant to use you. When you said that your dad was meeting with Principal Chromwell, I knew you were getting transferred.

I was scared of what that meant; I wanted us to do something memorable together. The portal had been on my mind for a few days and, well, one thing led to another."

"I want to do something meaningful too. I want to help our friends who got hurt protecting me. You read me Kohl's information, but what happened with Solei? Obviously, I've seen the end result, but I don't know how it started."

"After the mist, they had a hard time disconnecting from your mind. Honestly, they shouldn't have done it, but I'm in no place to judge risky decisions. When you lost your ear piece, Solei overreacted. They could see Diablo and Delphine in the fountain. The scene looked pretty gruesome. River water from the underworld looks a lot like blood, which is probably not coincidental now that I think about it. Anyway, Solei was convinced you were going to die. They tried to push the connection harder to find a way to talk to you. I think the goal was to communicate telepathically, but it splintered their mind. They couldn't find their way back to themself once you were safe. They were constantly having migraines; their electricity was harder to control. I was trying to handle their care myself, but I got in over my head. I couldn't even bring them into Ward B myself. Nadea and Principal Chromwell had to handle it. If I could get Solei to focus on me during one of their attacks, I think I could walk them back to where they need to be, but I can't get them to see past their pain."

"Wait, I actually think I can help with that. How often does Solei regain consciousness?"

Airess calculated the outbursts. "Every five hours or so?"

"Then we have about four hours to figure out how these work." Lena opened her bag and handed Airess the glasses.

Chapter 8
Care and Caution

Lena and Airess' experimentation with the glasses was a success. They took turns eliciting strong emotions from within and traveling to different locations. They knew using these glasses on Solei could do more harm than good if they couldn't guide their mind back home. The girls spent hours rehearsing how to leave the illusions they created, and how to pull the other back into reality. In the end, it felt rather instinctual.

"Ready to go back?" Lena asked.

"Yeah, let me grab the balm I made for Kohl and we can go." Airess pushed a cart out from the corner and filled it with canisters, murky vials, and potted flowers.

Airess guided their way out. Ward B was back to its usual stillness. They put the chair back in place for Lena and Airess started to treat Kohl while they waited.

"Nurse!" The siren was calling out to Airess. "Your friend has dried mud on them."

Lena was confused at first. Of course Solei would have dried mud on them. That was kind of the point.

Airess pretended to knock over a cup of water. "Silly me! I'm always dropping something!" She bent down and made haste to scrub the mud off Lena's cloak. She nodded to Delphine.

The front doors to the building opened. In walked Principal Chromwell, another adult Lena didn't recognize, Ms. Galen, and Kasim. They were there to see Kohl. Airess moved around the patient's bed to block Lena.

"Good evening, Miss Hikona. I assume you and yours are doing well?" Principal Chromwell was always so formal.

"Good evening, Headmistress! We're as well as we can be! Good evening, Professor Vontari, Mr. Basil!" Airess was her usual chipper self.

"Were you able to retrieve the vials of poison I requested?" Professor Vontari was inspecting the vials on the cart.

"I collected as many as I could without risking contamination from other fluids. I hope there's enough!" the bubble gum healer responded proudly.

Lena was so enthralled by the conversations that she missed that her dad had been staring directly at her the entire time. His face was tense. Lena offered a small wave behind the cloak. He rolled his eyes.

"Everything alright, Kasim?" inquired Principal Chromwell.

"Of course. Shall we get started?" He pulled a cloth pouch from the inside of his jacket.

Airess placed a hand over Kohl's chest protectively. "What's that?" She tried to sound supportive.

"Don't worry." Kasim retrieved an exquisite amulet from the small bag. The frame was composed of baroque style metal which encapsulated a clear crystal. "The plan is to have Kohl wear this around his neck and the gypsum will pull toxins from his body. Once the gem is no longer clear, it'll need to be removed and cleansed. We can repeat this process as many times as needed with few to no negative effects." He gave the necklace to Airess. "If my daughter were here, she'd want you to be the one to give this to him."

"I see. That settles it then, doesn't it? I can trust you will have this handled, Miss Hikona?" Principal Chromwell seemed perturbed.

"I will! I won't let you down!" Airess clenched the amulet to her heart in earnest.

With a nod, Kasim and Professor Vontari exited the ward.

"Ensure that you don't. I have no interest in you all causing any more of a ruckus." The principal gave a stern look to both girls.

"Best of luck with all your endeavors. Godspeed."

Airess waited until the room was cleared. "Phew! That was scary." She resumed caring for Kohl and adorning him with his new necklace.

Lena took off her mom's blanket. No point in invisibility now, her dad and P.C. knew exactly where she was.

"Hey. You're that girl, aren't you?"

Lena turned towards Delphine. "Me?"

"From the courtyard?"

Lena walked over. "Yeah, hey. I'm Lena."

"Hi Lena, I'm Delphine. I've heard a lot about you. Thanks for finding me, he said you would."

Lena stared blankly at the siren. *What?*

Solei's monitor started to beep.

"It's go time!" Airess shifted her care from Kohl to Solei.

"On it!" Lena retrieved the glasses. "Who should put the glasses on?"

"My hands are going to be pretty occupied, do you mind? We should wait until they start to open their eyes, but we need to make progress before their thrashing fit starts. The glasses won't hold during that. "

"Sure thing." Lena slid an arm of the glasses through the top of her shirt and bent down to whisper to her friend. "Solei, it's me. Airess thinks you might still be searching for our connection. I'm right here. Follow my voice."

"Lena...." Solei gasped as the lights flickered.

"Mhmm. Come look." Lena slid the glasses over Solei's face. They opened their eyes.

"See? Lena's right here and I've got your power completely under control, as promised. Legacy's all safe." Airess was trying to guide their thoughts to control the scene the glasses would create.

"Safe." The room was warming up. Their eyes were glazed but staying open. "Lucifer."

"Nope, no devils! Only good things here!" Airess panicked slightly.

"Devil? No devil!" Solei yelled and lightning bolts danced across their skin. Airess was trying to convince them Diablo didn't exist, but Lena understood Solei's strong reaction. Seeing Diablo had a huge impact on Lena, how could it not have done the same to Solei when they shared the same headspace?

Lena picked up Solei's hand and placed it on her face. Familiar jolts of pain touched her skin. Airess tried to protest but was overwhelmed moderating their friend's energy. "His name's Diablo. He saved us, Solei. Not with you, when it was just Airess and me. A boulder was coming straight at us; we weren't able to see it and he pushed us to safety."

Solei's body was still for a moment. "Good?"

"That's my impression. I ... I really feel for him, Solei. Regardless of whom he may or may not come from."

"Lucifer." Solei's voice was weak again, but the sparks had stopped.

"I was scared when I first met him too," Airess offered.

"He was quite the sight through the mist, wasn't he? All

flames and frustration. Not what we were expecting to find, huh?" The heat had died down.

"Angry. So angry." They sounded upset.

"He is always angry. He is also an unavoidable nuisance at times, but I've never seen him cruel or malicious." Airess made her disinterest clear.

"Devil's spawn or not, I'm choosing to give him a chance. A name is simply a name to me at this point. Nothing more." Lena reassured them. The monitor had stopped beeping. Airess replaced the glasses with the palms of her hands momentarily then released them.

"Just a name ... maybe ... just a name." Solei blinked and for the first time in over a week since their eyes had opened, they could finally see. "Airess! Lena!" The three friends wrapped together in a tight hug. "What are you doing here, Lena? I thought you'd be gone! Tao said you were getting transferred out."

"I did, but we can talk about that another time. How are you doing?! You gave us such a scare!"

"I'm ... overexerted." Solei was deliberate in their word choice. "But seeing you guys is worth it."

Airess had tears sliding down her face. "You have no idea how much it means to me to see you whole again."

They stayed there for a while together. All cramped on the tiny bed, not a one willing to move. Airess eventually called for Ms. Galen, but there was no expediency. When she came, Lena packed up to go.

Airess resumed her rounds, finishing with Kohl. "Hey! Check it out! It's working!" The once clear crystal had opaque strands swirling within. Airess was ecstatic as she explained the process to Ms. Galen and Solei. Ms. Galen's intrigue had her examining the amulet, while Solei was peacefully falling asleep.

"You did good today." Lena nudged her friend's shoulder.

"Couldn't have done it without you. You really came through."

Airess' compliment warmed Lena's heart.

They exchanged their goodbyes. Lena looked to talk to Delphine on her way out, but she was gone from her bed. Their conversation would certainly be a text to her friends later. Right now, it was time for Lena to go home to her family.

She re-enacted a play-by-play of her day the second she got through the door. She couldn't wait to share the great news. She only exaggerated a little and withheld the shortcomings of the blanket. The excitement was contagious. Kasim even gloated about his immunity to his own creations. Overall, her parents were proud.

They were happy for Lena's friend's recovery and grateful for the lack of danger. Kasim even let sneaking into Ward B slide when he realized Lena and her mom were in cahoots. Kamilah made dinner while playing right along with her role in the story and it turned out that bananas mixed with macaroni and cheese went surprisingly well together. The night was young, but Lena was exhausted. She checked her phone before bed. The group chat had been active.

"Miss me?" Solei had made their rallying known.

"Solei! My favorite surprises are the good ones I don't see beforehand! Excellent news."

"You should come visit. Little cub helped bring me back and Airess hasn't left my side since waking me up. Plus, there's a siren across from me that does not stop talking. You're perfect for each other!"

Airess replied with an onslaught of hug emojis.

"Sorry your sense of humor hasn't changed. Oops. Autocorrect." Tao did not shy away from his regular banter with Solei.

"Clever as ever! I rhyme now too. Whatcha gonna do?"

Oh my.

"I'll swing by after dinner. I've missed this."

Lena debated texting about what Delphine said, but she didn't want to come across as attention seeking. She decided to show her appreciation instead. "Enjoy your visit, Tao! Ten out of ten recommend. Love you guys. Goodnight."

Sleep came quickly. Lena dreamt of fiery gazes and warm embraces. Diablo's presence felt tangible. His skin shone like moonlight, his hair soft as a night-time breeze. She tried to memorize his every feature. Two pointed tips stuck out near his temples. She wanted to feel them. He was, by far, the most enthralling person she had ever laid eyes upon. Lena's heart leapt every time he was near;

she was entranced. They walked along the clouds, hand in hand, until they reached a field. Closing the gap between them, he pointed out different constellations and told their stories. Lena mustered up enough courage to lay her head on his shoulder. His sudden stop made her worry. She had caught him off guard. Diablo wrapped his arm around her. Neither one of them were willing to break the silence. Two snow-white horses whinnied nearby, galloping in the wildflowers.

"I've never been close, like this, to a boy before."

"I've never been close, like this, to anyone before."

There was a long pause. Crickets chirped. The wind rustled the grass.

"It's nice being here with you." Lena nuzzled deeper into him. His clothing smelled singed. The smell reminded her of her dad's workshop.

"Then stay," Diablo offered.

She wanted that more than anything. If she could avoid waking up, she'd never have to leave. Life maintained other plans.

~~~~~~~~~~~~~~~~~~~~~~~~~~~

"Ms. Galen found a new portal in Ward A last night. Meet me downstairs in five." Kasim spoke through Lena's door.

Lena didn't want to wake up. She wanted to roll back over and fall asleep. She wanted to stay in the field. She knew that space was too far gone now to return to. *I suppose a new portal is exciting too.*

"Morning! How'd you sleep, Magpie?"

"Excellent. Yourself?"

"Pretty good, your mom's still out."

"She's been genuinely helpful the past few days."

"So have you, Lena. Your decision-making has really shown improvement. Theodora thinks that's true of your friends as well. She mentioned how great a team you all make and that you all remind her of the old days sometimes. In fact, that's why I brought up the portal. Principal Chromwell thinks we should all study it together."

"We get to go back to another portal? I've only had one lesson."

"Not in it, Lena. If I had my say, I'd never let you into another one again. It's too high of a risk, and honestly gods aren't worth it to me."

"I don't understand then."

"Before anyone jumps into an unknown realm, the portal should be examined intensely. Each part of the entryway gives a clue. With enough research, you could possibly figure out who you're trying to save in the first place which is paramount as not every god is good."

"I didn't think Ward A judged behavior. Shouldn't that be a job for someone like Anubis?"

"I acknowledge how you feel, but you haven't seen deities act the way I have, Lena. A majority want to engage in battle. You kids were lucky when you found Aglaope predominantly lamented."

Aglaope. "Aren't they being saved from extinction?"

"I have only encountered a small percentage of gods within this universe, but not a single one has ever been appreciative or kind.

Their atrociousness only scales from spiteful to torturous."

"Then why are you involved now if you detest the deities so much?"

"Because you're too much like your parents, Magpie; we never would have walked away at your age if we weren't forced to."

Lena gave her dad a small squeeze. "I want to help them, Dad. My friends, the gods, everyone."

"I know, sweetie. Gear up and we'll meet the team there."

Lena packed her bag. She tried to grab everything she envisioned being useful.

"All set?" Kamilah looked packed up too.

"Umm, Mom?" Lena looked for her dad. There was no way Kamilah joining them was a good idea.

"She wouldn't listen," Kasim's voice yelled from down the hall.

"If my family's going, I'm going." Kamilah was insistent.

"Mom, we go out all the time, it's fine. It's safer for you to stay home."

"Magdalena, you think it's acceptable for you to be involved in dangerous activities, but a grown adult, who has done this all before mind you, can't handle the same risks?"

Lena knew the answer was yes. She also knew not to answer that. "Dad!"

"It's no use. I've tried." He shrugged.

"Principal Chromwell's fine with this too?"

"Theodora loves me! We're ... what's the term? Oh, right. Besties!" Kamilah beamed.

"Theodora doesn't know." Kasim informed his daughter.

"I think she'll probably figure it out, Dad, don't you?"

He jingled the car keys. "I've got the keys, let's roll!"

Kamilah made a smug face. "You're all so concerned about me and he thinks you roll a car to get it to move. Ridiculous."

Lena took a deep breath and followed her mom out. She knew the portal was no longer going to be the most eventful part of her day, but on the plus side, she wasn't going to be the one getting into trouble this time. One of their favorite songs came on the radio as soon as they got into the car. They cranked the volume up too loud and sang the whole way to Legacy Academy. Their spirits were all pretty high by the time Airess came running out to their car.

"Mr. Basil! Lena! Mrs. Basil?"

"Mom, this is Airess. She's the one who takes care of Ina. She also works in Ward B."

"Oh Ina...." Kamilah glanced down and looked away. Not the reaction Lena was hoping for.

"I texted you like a million times! It's Kohl! He's awake!"

"That's fantastic, Ms. Hikona!"

"Yes! Well. Kinda. He's very ... normal? Which would be the goal if we weren't where we are. Does that make sense? I think I've been spending too much time with Principal Chromwell."

"He lost his powers? That's devastating." Lena compared Kohl to her mom.

"Right? I'm so glad you said that! That was my initial reaction too!"

"Sounds like Kohl may not feel that way?" Kasim was reading in between the lines.

"Not at all! Can you believe that?" Airess' deliverance was contemptuous, but it wasn't that shocking to Lena. He called his gifts a curse and shuddered when talking about them. Didn't Kohl say Airess tried to save him when they were in Aglaope's portal? Shouldn't she know more than anyone how much he loathed the talents he possessed?

"I'll go in and talk to him. Millie, want to join me?" She nodded and they went inside.

Lena held back. "Airess, didn't he hate his powers? I think we should be happy for him, shouldn't we?"

"Lena, everyone dislikes their relations with the gods sometimes. Even I complain about working at the wards periodically. That doesn't mean permanently losing what makes you special is a cause for celebration."

"I haven't had a lot of time with him, but I don't think his abilities ever made him feel special. He called them a curse more than anything; didn't he even drop out a few times to avoid using them?"

"I agree. You haven't had a lot of time with him, or in this world. I need to get back; Kohl needs me. You should join us too. There's a whole cluster of people inside."

Lena was taken aback. Airess' flip from hot to cold was immobilizing. Lena seriously considered leaving. Seeing Tao's taxi in the parking lot was enough to change her mind.

"Little cub!" Solei's voice boomed across the open room. "Get over here!"

Lena couldn't help but feel better. She went to sit on the edge of their bed beside Tao and watched the large group around Kohl. "Full house today, huh?"

"Everyone is freaking out; it's sort of hilarious honestly. They go from cheering to petrified in about half a second." Solei was legitimately eating popcorn while they watched.

"Solei is running for humanitarian of the year, can you tell?" Tao enjoyed his banter. "How are you, Lena? It's been a minute."

"Things are going well. I'm happy."

"You? Happy? Maybe the world has turned upside down."

"Tao Vovi, Astoria's premier cynic, everybody." Solei chaffed.

"I'm not a cynic. I simply have opinions and a strong will to express them."

"Hear, hear," teased Lena. "What's all the buzz about anyway?"

Solei was eager to answer. "Everyone gathered here early this morning when Ward A reported the portal. P.C., a few teachers I didn't recognize, Ms. Galen, and that one guy that's obsessed with Kohl's poison."

"Professor Vontari? He's a genius. I didn't see him when I came in earlier." Tao was disappointed.

"P.C. wanted to check the amulet before leaving, it was completely opaque. Kohl woke up right when Airess pulled the necklace off. Trouble was that he was visibly different; he looked so full of life. A few more people were called in, but it was pretty obvious he wasn't undead anymore."

"Wow, that's huge. I had no idea. I heard from Airess his reaction wasn't what she expected."

The invisibility and fear of the dead made more sense to Lena now.

"I walked in on that. Who knew an entire building could feel so awkward simultaneously?" Tao raised his eyebrows.

"I'm not sure why Airess blew up. Kohl's had so many implosions and explosions when training. He's nice enough, but I was never sure how he'd react to anything. That kid has always been a loose cannon." Solei sounded resigned.

Can't say his relationship with Airess wasn't founded on commonality.

"Solei, right?" Kasim stood beside the group.

"Mr. Basil! What an honor."
They sat upright, pushing Lena and
Tao off the bed by proxy.

Kasim laughed. "I don't know
about all that. I'm heading to the
portal and I heard you might be kind
enough to help me."

"I've never been to Ward A."
They sounded disappointed. "I'm all
for helping though! Whatever you
need!"

"That's good enough for me.
How about all of you?" Kasim
looked to his wife, Lena, and Tao.

"I always need all the help I can
get," Kamilah said with a straight
face.

"Then off we go!" Kasim made sure Solei could walk without assistance and led the charge.

Solei leaned down to Lena. "Your mom is adorable, little cub." Lena had to agree.

"Do you think we should've invited Airess?" Tao whispered.

Lena was about to shake her head no when her father answered. "I invited Ms. Hikona to join us. She vigorously declined."

They traversed Ward A. All the hallways were the same to Lena— sterile and banal. Kasim, and surprisingly Kamilah, seemed to notice a plethora of distinguishing factors in the long halls. Lena's mom marveled at all the new changes; Kasim shared jokes about aged memories. Both shared their tips and advice from their time at Ward A. Their tour was enjoyable, but none of their tricks were innate.

"I can smell the portal; they all have their own smell if you take the time to discern it," Kasim instructed.

"It smells like cinder mixed with spoiled food." Lena scrunched her nose.

"Maybe the doorway had fruit that didn't last? Does godly fruit spoil?" Solei was keen to see their first portal. "Found it!"

The magical gateway was mesmerizing. Intricate bows formed the arched frame. At the crest, there were soft pillow-like clouds. Above the white puffs shone a heavenly golden light; below a storm manifested. Streaks of bright lightning lit up the scene. Grey accents flowed along the base of the clouds causing rain to pour down onto the ground. Rivers formed from those droplets and carried the water back into the door's depths. The door itself was made of ivory. Etchings of an elephant transformed before the group. First, a robust head with five trunks protruded towards them. Then the trunks withdrew and the mammal gained ten tusks. Lastly, the tusks faded away and five elephant heads emerged to cover the broad entryway.

Tao was running his finger along the bows. "I would need Professor Vontari to confirm, but based on the carvings, I believe these are astras."

"Astras?" Lena moved closer for a better view.

"They're supernatural weapons in Hinduism. They're one of the first magical items I heard about. A deity would endow certain powers onto them to make them unrivaled by any normal means." Solei was inspecting the other bow.

"They feel tricky; I don't like their energy." Kamilah had taken a step back.

"They are Mrs. Basil, without a doubt. They have a lot of rules and circumstances to follow if someone wants to wield them. Missing even the smallest detail could result in a painful death for the user. They're very tricky," Solei added.

"Unless you're the god that created them," Kasim countered.

"If this is a god who has an astra, that greatly limits our scope of possibilities. It also means they can kill us with minimal effort and there isn't anything that can protect us, correct?" Tao's voice revealed that he was unnerved.

Lena wondered if Aglaope's doorway would've sounded as bleak had Airess analyzed its components beforehand. "What do we do now, Dad?"

"I'll text Theodora, but now we wait. Once we join forces with her lot, we can brainstorm as a larger body and form educated guesses to research later."

A few members of the group seemed restless.

"I've gotten some of my best ideas while meditating; want to try it with me?" Tao offered.

"That's a great idea. Millie, come join me?" Kasim held out his hand and Millie mimicked the action, offering her hand to Solei. The three sat on the ground and let Tao guide them into a peaceful meditation. Lena found a spot against the wall and simply stared at the portal.

What was she going to do against lethal bows and an angry mutating elephant during a rainstorm?

Chapter 9
Shock and Surprise

As Tao expected, Professor Vontari's insights were priceless. He spoke to the group about the astras endlessly. Tao was captivated by the professor's presence. Principal Chromwell helped redirect him to the rest of the portal's decor to hypothesize possible inhabitants.

Principal Chromwell, Professor Vontari, Tao, Kasim, and Solei were flooded with ideas and spent hours deliberating. Another professor had joined the group; they referred to her as Dr. Palaios. She researched their suggestions while also offering her input. At one point, Lena's mom fell asleep listening to their discussion. Lena wanted to too. The talks were interesting to a point, but after too long she started to zone out. She wished Airess had joined them. Despite her snippiness earlier, it would've been nice to spend time with a friend. Lena also kept a keen eye out for Diablo. She had no idea what she would do if she saw him, but that didn't reduce her enthusiasm.

"That solves it then. We've agreed on who we're up against. We will spend the night doing our designated research and send our findings to Dr. Palaios. Tomorrow, after she's compiled our data, we will train. Agreed?" The vote was unanimous, though Lena missed what she was agreeing to.

Principal Chromwell approached Kamilah. "Millie, would you be up for spending the evening together?"

"I suppose I would be awake if we spent the evening together." She turned to Kasim for his input.

He hid his shock quickly and gave a smile of encouragement. "How are you feeling?"

"Rested."

Principal Chromwell interjected. "Let me rephrase my

question. Would you like to join me for dinner, Millie?"

"Can Ina join us?" Kamilah gently asked.

"Oh, sweetie, she—" Kasim tried to explain.

Principal Chromwell raised her hand and cut him off. "Of course, but she will likely not be up for it. Will her sleeping bother you?"

"No. People are usually calm in their sleep."

"I concur. Ina is serene. We'll share dinner together then?" P.C. pushed.

"Have her home safely by eight?" Kasim was clearly uncomfortable.

"I promise to treat her with the utmost care, Kasim. I'll be happy to deliver her back home when we're done tonight."

Even Lena knew that answer evaded what her dad asked. His face masked all emotion. "I am choosing to trust you, Theodora." His voice was firm.

"Of course you are! We all trust one another! We're T.A.A.!" Kamilah went to form a group hug with Kasim and Theodora.

"We most certainly are. Nothing will ever change that, Millie." Principal Chromwell shot a glare at Kasim. "Now, let's go find some food to cook."

"Oh! Is it hidden? I always enjoy a good challenge!"

"I do find determining dinner to be an elusive process." Out the two friends went.

Lena rested her head on her dad's shoulder. "On a scale from one to ten, how difficult was that for you?"

"One hundred, but a certain young lady is teaching me to give my loved ones space."

"If it helps, I don't think you had a choice."

"It doesn't and I did not." Her dad admitted his defeat.

"Never fear! I have our night all planned out already!"

"Oh do you? That was quick."

"I have a great hypothetical situation for us to work through about the entryway we all studied!" Lena exclaimed.

"I'm impressed, Magpie. I didn't think you were paying attention."

"That may or may not be relevant to my hypothetical situation."

Kasim laughed. "Say it is, what would be the inquiry posed?"

"I'm thinking something along the lines of: Who is believed to be inside said magical doorway and what is our designated research?"

"To be clear, the hypothetical situation would be: What was the whole point to that several hours' long discussion?"

"AND what are we supposed to do now? The shortened version though. I love a good highlight reel." Lena was intentionally teasing at this point.

"What am I going to do with you?" He led the way back to their car.

"Teach me everything you know!"

"Including information you were already present for?"

"Especially information I was already present for! People actually expect me to know those things!" Lena's smile was wide.

"I am one of those people, Lena."

"Dad, we've been at this for fourteen years. I'd like to believe you know me better than that by now."

Amused, Kasim drove them home. If his missing Kamilah wasn't already apparent, his creation of french fry stuffed tacos for dinner confirmed it. Lena tried to keep their conversations light and vaguely silly, which was hard considering the deity assumed to be within the portal was referred to as "The King of the Highest Heavens."

"Two thoughts, Dad. One: why does a king of gods have a portal in Ward A? Two: at what point does it make any sense for us to go up against a king of gods?"

"Based on my understanding, Indra fell out of favor due to many misdeeds and may have also been cursed by another god. The latter is harder to prove."

"Please correct me, and tell me if I'm wrong, but he's presumably a cursed king of gods with superpowered bows that nothing our world can do anything against?"

"Yeah. I think that sums it up well. Back to your second question, I think portals are a horrible idea. We've discussed that."

"If Vontari knew Indra's name so readily, how is he forgotten?"

"That's actually an insightful question, Lena. Followers of Hinduism are discouraged from worshiping this particular deity. It's not that they don't believe in him, it's that they aren't devoted to him."

"That can't be right. Lack of attention cannot be enough to cause their eternal deterioration. Can it?"

"If it can't, I'm not sure why Indra would be in Ward A. Gods are typically rather vain, no matter what religion they're aligned to. I wouldn't be surprised if the catalyst in question is not that he has no followers but that he doesn't have enough." Kasim loathed the supreme beings. Lena kept her disagreement hushed. She was skeptical of their suspected god; he seemed too high of value to be fading away.

Their assigned topic of research for the night was the astras. Putting Kasim in charge of magical items made sense to Lena. They discovered Indra had designed at least five different astras. Most were believed to have a one-time use, but the descriptions were not always so concise. There was a possible silver lining to their digging. A majority of Indra's known astras were handed down to his son. Lena hoped if his son was not present, maybe the astras would not be either. Kasim's opinion was not swayed. He perpetually assumed the worst of these situations.

Lena was struggling to keep her eyes open. Her dad gave her an out and sent her to bed. She gave him a hug and headed upstairs. She had been eager to reconvene with her pillow since she had awakened. She drifted off to sleep easily.

~~~~~~~~~~~~~~~~~~~~~~~~~~~~~~

Lena's dreams were uneventful to say the least and it had put her in a grumpy mood. She had to be up early for the meeting, but she wanted to stay home like her mom. The previous group from Ward A, plus a few extras, were gathered on Legacy's field. Among the new teammates were Airess and Kohl. Dr. Palaios was giving a presentation on all the information. It felt rather repetitive. Lena wanted to see the magical items her dad and Solei had put together then get to the hands-on portion of the meeting.

Principal Chromwell began her presentation. "It is with great pride that I am able to see you all answering the call of Ward A. It has been decades since such a team was formed. I am honored to be included in both. May your journeys afar bring you closer to home and your hearts never wander from your core truths. Doctor Palaios, your information has been grandly enlightening. We all thank you for that. By the day's end, I shall pick a team of five for retrieval. The extraction shall be performed this weekend. I wish many blessings onto all of you and good tidings for the future. Thank you all. We will now be moving on to the practical skills portion of the day. For that, I offer a jovial welcome to Mr. Basil and his new apprentice, Solei."

One day, Lena thought, *she will speak and I will understand her. That will be a good day. Also, when did Solei become my dad's apprentice?*

"Hi everybody, it's been a long morning; we want to keep this short. We've made blueprints for three different options for the rescuers to bring in as well as one item we'd like everyone to have. Once the team is decided, they can let us know what they'd like and we'll get to customizing their items. Without further ado, the first item we wanted to make was a shield. If all our information is correct, Indra's temperament is more aggressive than passive. Moreover, he likely has a giant almighty elephant. We wanted to be able to offer our rescuers a line of defense. Solei, do you mind demonstrating?"

Solei stepped forward with an arm across their chest. There was a thick banded bracelet around their wrist. The center was a circle with a design too far away to make out. They made a pounding motion with their fist and went down to one knee. An iridescent dome surrounded them.

"This is a grounding shield. When the correct movements are applied, it will jut into the ground and block its user. This is beneficial both for stabilizing your position and using the ground's natural elements to subdue the anticipated electrical attacks. It will provide cover from rain too, but that should not be used as its primary function. It is not permanent; not much I offer will be. The shield can last for roughly three heavy attacks or ten minutes."

"Does that include attacks from an astra?" Tao asked.

"Nothing will include attacks from an astra. The only defense against those are fleeing or luck even the gods would envy."

The crowd was silenced temporarily.

"Moving on. Next, we have a staff. While the shield aims to negate electrical damage, this steers right into it. The handles are made of a dense wood for safety, but the weapon itself is made of bronze. Bronze is a highly conductive metal. We've also added specks of iron and nickel to make it slightly magnetic. We cannot create anything as strong as a god's powers, but we can use their powers against them. This aims to harness any electricity he passes to us and send it back with a little extra umph. Solei?"

They gave a small wooden cylinder a fast shake and dazzling

bronze extensions protruded from both ends. Solei's movements were hypnotizing. They were a whirlwind of copper and lightning. Their war dance was flawless. They exuded power. Lena stared in wonderment.

"The last item we have is a bit more complicated. We're calling it the Ring of Prana. The bearer of this ring will be able to breathe underwater, but it must also be accompanied by an herbal supplement. Ms. Hikona has been kind enough to cultivate the areca palm for us. With simultaneous usage, the user should be able to remain submerged for hours without any qualms."

"What happens if you only have the ring?" Professor Vontari inquired.

"We believe the abilities would remain the same but in a significantly less stable manner. Whoever dons the ring should carry both items to ensure their safety."

Solei was now sporting thick clunky rubber boots and being a slight distraction.

"Ah yes, our last recommendation. Rubber boots! They're uncomfortable, but I strongly suggest you wear them anyway. They are an excellent insulator, so they'll be able to prevent electrocution from any supercharged water you could be trekking through. Additionally, bites from any surprise creature encounters would also be dulled." Kasim was talking about what happened to Kohl and they all knew it.

"These are a part of your magical item roster?" Dr. Palaios was scrolling through her tablet, surely looking for them on her list.

"Nope. They're just common sense. That's about it for our part. I'll be here for any questions; otherwise, good luck training, everyone!"

The adults began to cluster around Kasim. Lena's friends went out into the field. Lena straggled behind. Solei was demonstrating the shield and staff again. The whole group seemed to be laughing and having a good time. Lena attempted to join in the fun. Her spirit meant well, but she was struggling. In an effort to help, Solei convinced her to try out the shield while Tao hit Solei's bolts into it with the staff.

"Act like you're going to punch the ground and crouch, okay? We won't send anything your way until you're all set up. Ready? I'll count you in. One. Two. Three."

Lena did as instructed and crouched under the protective bubble. The shield blocked out everything. The world became quiet and undisturbed. Lena noticed her friends waiting on her, she gave a thumbs up. Solei gestured for her to stay still and wait while they worked with Tao on hitting their sparks in a controlled manner. Lena scanned the field. All of her friends were engrossed in their training. She wondered who would be picked. Lena glimpsed a light from the corner of her eye. She wanted to be prepared for the incoming hits; she planted her feet firmly and turned back to Tao. Lena's gaze was met with flames instead of lightning bolts. She tried to yell, "Diablo!" but her breath caught and what she got out sounded like, "No!" That was right before Tao hit a lightning bolt square at Lena's chest. The jolt met with a loud crack and sent her flying across the field.

Lena's head hurt from the landing, but her body felt okay. She could hear a commotion a few feet away, but the sounds were muddled. She sat up. Her view into the field was hazy, but she could see the grass stains on her shoes just fine. She inspected her clothes for scorch marks, but there weren't any.

"You were lucky to be saved, sweet child. The powers of Lucifer are great indeed." A voice echoed from above.

Lena searched her small perimeter. The grass below was covered with glowing streaks. Her eyes burned looking straight at them. "Hello?"

"Up here, young one. I've been waiting for you longer than anticipated. Are you slow, child?"

Confused, Lena peered into the sky. It was a perfect shade of bright blue. She thought she could see the breeze at first, but upon closer scrutiny it was billowing fabric. A trumpet appeared before her, held afloat by golden sparkles.

"I said, 'Are you slow, child?' Do you require aid?"

"No. I don't think so. I don't understand. What's happening? Who are you? Where are you?"

"Ah. I've seen this before. Mortals can take a while to process my presence. Concerning the topic of my name, I have many. Many names, many faces. Your mother referred to me as Jibril, but you may call me Gabriel. I am everywhere. I am also nowhere. To some, I am revered with the utmost reverence and to others I lack existence in its entirety. My travels, particularly to this plane, are minimal. I am present only when my merciful God requests it."

"I've heard your name before, but I don't remember your story."

"That's because your parents are blasphemous. The Basil name has no bloodline. Your moniker is falsified. The only truth your family holds is within the centuries your ancestors devoted to their unrelenting claim to Allah's name. You descend from a long line of sacrilege to me."

Kasim's disdain was making more sense to Lena. "I have no

desire to argue with you, but my love for my parents is unchanged."

"I'm not here to change your mind. My purpose is to enlighten. For you are now my own as well. You are my chosen Legacy."

Of all the things the entity Jibril could have said, Lena least expected that one. "Wait, what?"

"Do me proud, young one. Bear my name with honor. Defend what deserves defending. Godspeed."

Lena's mouth was agape when the angel's glow dimmed and the hazy barrier dropped.

"Little cub!" Solei basically tackled a sitting Lena checking her over. "What hurts? Where did it hit? Why did you retract the shield?"

Lena stared at her friend, mute. "There aren't any marks. I heard the bolt hit. Why aren't there any marks?" Solei turned to face Airess for answers.

"The rings must have restored her physical state back to normal. I've never seen them activate up close like that. Lena, what did you see? What did it feel like?" Airess was awestruck.

"I thought they were only a rumor. I didn't think the rings ever actually activated," Tao remarked in astonishment.

"Solei, you should probably call her dad over. She doesn't look right." Kohl was standing some distance away observing the scene. Solei rapidly obliged. Kasim had seen the golden light of the rings but never guessed it was Lena who activated them. He took her home and laid her in bed straight away. Lena's dreams were impatiently waiting to welcome her.

~~~~~~~~~~~~~~~~~~~~~~~~~~

Lena found herself instantly swept up into a seaside cave. The air smelt like saltwater. The waves crashed to a hypnotic melody. The moon reflected pristinely off the distant waters.

"I was worried you wouldn't come." Diablo spoke softly behind her.

"I'm not sure why you'd think that." She reached for his hand.

"You're the elusive one of the two of us."

He intertwined his fingers with hers. "I'm not used to … people. But I like how it feels being with you."

Butterflies consumed her belly. *Be calm. He's not real.* She met his gaze. *If I screamed how I felt, would you reject me in my own dream?* "There's no place I'd rather be."

Diablo's pale cheeks blushed. "How are you feeling after today? That was pretty intense."

"Oh my gosh. You have no idea! I met a god! Who does that?!" Lena remembered all his sign-ins at Ward A. "Well, other than you. You always seem to be the exception."

"Heh. I've heard that a time or two. It's not usually a compliment." He walked out onto the moonlit shore.

Ouch. That went poorly. Come back! "I didn't mean it as an insult. I wouldn't change a thing about you." Lena sat next to him and laid her head on his shoulder. He flinched.

"Wouldn't you though? People take one look at me, judge me, then spend the rest of their time trying to fix whatever they deem is wrong with me."

"Hey. Come on now. When have I ever done any of that?" She moved in front of him.

"Never. That's the problem." He was trying to hide his tears.

"It's a problem to like you based on actual interactions with you?" She wiped his hair away from his face.

"It is because it'll hurt that much more when things change."

Her hands touched the points on his head. She followed the curve. Lena gasped. "Diablo, you're not.... Those aren't...." Lena traced the shape of a crescent one more time just to be sure. "That's a moon. Those aren't horns." She stared at him aghast. His face remained neutral. "You're related to a moon deity. You're not related to the devil at all."

"Unless I say I am." His voice was void of inflection.

"What? Why would you do that? You're not Diablo."

"If I answer to a name, then it's an identity I'm choosing. My heritage is irrelevant at that point."

"It's so relevant! We should tell people! They have it all wrong!"

"Not a chance. Why should the people who've called me names and harassed me my whole life get anything from me?"

"If they know the truth, maybe they can change!"

"Can't you see that they've already made their decisions? I don't have anything to do with that."

"You should come to Legacy with me!" She reached out to his

shoulders. He flinched again, harder. Her right hand came back sticky. It was covered in blood.

Diablo lifted his shirt off his back. "I'm already at Legacy more often than I'd like to be these days." He had a deep gaping wound with lightning bolt edges along his back. "I got to you without a second to spare. I tried to get us both out of the way, but hitting the barrier of those rings was like a brick wall for me."

"We need to get you to Ward B."

"I can heal here."

"I'll take you, please come with me." Lena's anxiety was rising.

"It's not that easy, Lena."

"It is. Let's go." She pulled at him.

"Stay. Please." He was begging.

"Come on, Diablo!"

"Don't do this...."

"I want to go now!"

"I thought there was nowhere else you wanted to be?"

"If I can't help you get better, then I want to wake up. Watching you in pain is too much, even in a dream."

"If you don't want me in pain, then stay. Losing you is far worse than any laceration."

Lena closed her eyes. *Wake up, wake up, wake up!*

"Lena. Don't."

Lena awoke sweaty. It was 3:10 a.m. Her face was tearstained; her throat was sore. Her night terror had taken quite the physical toll. She watched the waning moon outside her bedroom window, yearning to trace the lines of Diablo's face in actuality.

Chapter 10
Plans and Prejudices

"The list is out, have you seen it?" Kasim was preparing breakfast for the family.

Principal Chromwell's crew announcement had completely slipped Lena's mind. She picked up her phone and swiped away all the spoiler notifications from her friends.

"My dearest champions, it is with a full heart I

compose this message. The bravery of Ward A's candidates has blown me away. Your proficiencies and strength are truly worthy of the gods, which I am grateful for as that is precisely the caliber required for the task at hand. While any combination of participants would likely triumph, I believe the quintet I have chosen below possess the strongest aptitude towards our anticipated rival. Without further ado, I implore the following individuals to join

<u>Operation: Heavenly Champion</u>

Professor Vontari

Doctor Palaios

Airess Hikona

Solei

Magdalena Basil"

There she was. Her name was clear as day. Her father's name, however, was absent.

"You're not on it?" Lena looked up to him in the kitchen.

"Nah. I didn't want to be either, if I'm being honest." He served her a plate of eggs.

"But you've done this before. You have the most experience out of everyone. How could you not be on the team?"

"Well Magpie, I assume the first way is not to get picked," Kasim playfully teased his daughter trying to lighten the mood.

Lena shook her head at the open message on her phone. "It doesn't feel right."

"You'll do great, Lena, and even if I'm not on the team it doesn't mean I can't be with you."

"Really?" Her voice was small; she didn't want to admit she was scared.

He raised her chin so her eyes met his. "There is nothing in this world that can keep me from protecting you and your mother. No god, no principal, nothing. You will always have me."

Lena wrapped her arms around him in a big hug.

"Now, go get ready. Theodora expects you on the field in less than an hour."

Lena hurriedly finished eating and went upstairs. Her head was swimming. She was trying to process everything about the expedition ahead of her, but her heart kept pulling her back to last night. She couldn't decide which hurt more: finding out the name Diablo was fake or having to hear how his voice sounded when he last called out to her. Who knew dreams could be so cruel? Even if his presence was a figment of her imagination, the pain was incredibly realistic.

Lena did her best going through the motions to get to the field on time. The car ride was hushed and she was half present as she walked up to the crowd.

"It's gone! Everything is gone!" Airess screamed.

"Hysterics have never solved anything, Ms. Hikona. Please take a second and compose yourself. Solei, is there anywhere else you can think of where these items could be? Perhaps they're simply misplaced instead of stolen? I imagine that's a much more likely scenario, do you not?"

"Normally I'd agree with you, Principal Chromwell, but I think I messed up. There was a lot of excitement yesterday over the rings and I'm not sure I put them in safe keeping. I don't remember leaving them out, but I don't remember putting them away either."

"I see. I think it's probably time we call Mr. Basil then. Ah! Here comes Lena. Miss, is your father with you perchance?"

Lena was caught off guard. "Umm. No." There was a long pause. No one took their gaze off of her. "Sorry?"

Principal Chromwell raised her hand in dismissal. "Fret not. I'll be in my chambers until further notice looking into this. I trust you can handle training despite our vast magical loss, Professor Vontari?"

"Yes ma'am. You can count on me." He turned to the crowd. "Please join me by the goal post for a tale of debauchery and pride!"

The groans of the group were audible. Airess pulled Lena back.

"Hey, I wanted to check in with you. Yesterday was really something!"

"You have no idea." Lena was getting caught up in her own thoughts again.

Airess reached for her friend's hands. "What's wrong?"

Realizing what was happening, Lena moved away. "Nothing. Everything's fine."

Airess scowled. "That's clearly not the case." She reached again for Lena's hands.

"You know, it's not right to use your powers on other people whenever you want, Airess. You should get consent first."

The shade of the healer's face started to match her bubble gum hair. "At least I have powers to use! I help people!"

That one hurt. "I'm not doing this with you today. I don't have it in me. Enjoy your story time, Airess." Lena tried to go, but she felt resistance against her shoulders. Then she heard a whisper in her ear.

"Stay." Diablo's voice was unmistakable.

Lena's heart ached for him. "Diablo." She reached out to feel his touch.

"Diablo?" Airess asked. Solei was there too now. Lena was tearing up.

"I noticed you guys never made it to Indra's tales of woe over there. What's going on?"

"I think she's associating with the devil," Airess commented in a snotty tone.

Lena gave her a disgusted look. "Do you even hear yourself sometimes? Solei, it's Diablo. I'm worried he's severely hurt and not getting help. I also think there's a possibility he's not who he says he is either."

"Sounds like something a devil would do." Airess spoke directly to Solei.

"Airess, take a breath." Agitated, Solei did the same. Then they motioned for Tao to come over. He didn't look very pleased to be leaving his learning session. "Lena, what are you thinking?"

Was it safe to tell them? She wasn't sure any of them were ready to see Diablo like she did. "I have these dreams."

"Enlightening." Tao was indeed crabby.

Lena ignored him. "I see Diablo in them sometimes. I know dreams aren't real life, but I think these hold some truth. It's like my mind takes everything I saw during the day and organizes it for me so it makes sense later. Take yesterday for example, I pulled up the shield because I SWORE I saw him. Then, in my dream last night, he had wounds from Solei's bolt on his back."

"He was here yesterday?" Airess was irate.

Choosing to ignore her, Lena continued. "We got into a fight over all of it. He needs medical attention, but I couldn't get him to listen." Her breath was catching. She looked towards Solei. "I need him to be okay."

"Little cub." Solei wrapped their friend in a hug. "I'm sure he'll figure it out. I don't know Diablo well, but he seems resourceful from what I've seen."

Wiping away her tears, Lena concurred. "Yeah, I guess so."

"Tao, did you have any visions about Diablo?" Airess pressed.

"You know I'm not into talking about my visions."

"Tao, a group of us are about to go into a portal and all of our curated magical defenses are gone. I think if you have something, now's a good time to share it, especially if you saw Diablo steal everything after his little moment with Lena, don't you think?"

"Airess." Solei looked shocked.

Tao nodded in agreement. "That's quite a statement there, Airess."

"She has a mouthful of them," Lena said under her breath.

"I heard that. Lena, I've seen your feelings for him, but you're ignoring some blatantly obvious facts. Hardly anyone knows about our training and none of us took them. It's not that hard to put together the odd one out. Not to mention how convenient it is that he, by your own words Lena, happened to already be deceitful. All signs point to Diablo being the thief." Airess' face showed arrogance and her tone dripped condescension.

Solei sighed. "I don't necessarily agree with how she's gone about this Lena, but Airess does have a point. I've felt your feelings towards him too, but the training here is literally under wraps. I helped put a veil of deception over the field and all the attendees yesterday. Your dad and I checked this area from multiple angles to make sure the illusion worked before we went down for our presentation. If Diablo got in, he either had to be on the field before we finished or be able to get past our magic. Neither possibility errs in his favor."

"Lena, do you know why we're never able to see Diablo?" Tao was making an effort to help.

Lena had never really thought of it. "No." She wanted to come up with something to defend her case, to defend Diablo. "I am confident he has a good heart though. Doesn't that mean something?" she asked Tao.

He was perplexed. "Man, I don't know, Lena. I mean, yes, I get with your talents how that's relevant, but also, no. You haven't begun any studies—"

Airess cut him off. "Exactly. So, we agree then, right? Diablo is the one who took everything."

Lena scanned the room; no one would make eye contact with her or Airess. Solei eventually conceded to the posed accusation. Tao simply huffed and shook his head. That was enough for the healer to feel vindicated in her judgments. It was also enough for Lena to gauge the loyalty of the group.

"Can we get back to Professor Vontari? I hate all of this drama." Tao was slowly walking away.

"I couldn't agree more." Lena stalked off, far away from her so-called friends.

~~~~~~~~~~~~~~~~~~~~~~~~~~~

Lena obeyed her instructors but kept to herself. She tried to practice her sight during the downtime; she focused on the wind and the air attempting to pick up anything that seemed like a signal. She wanted to clear Diablo's name, that was true, but she also wanted to find out who took the items her dad and Solei had worked so hard on. She had no intention of entering another portal defenseless again. There were times, Lena acknowledged, when she wasn't sure she wanted to enter another portal again period. Legacy Academy was so overwhelming, but Ward A was monumentally more formidable.

Lena wished she had a support network to fall back on. She felt so isolated lately. Airess acted like a loose cannon, Solei kept siding with opposing opinions, Tao had impenetrable boundaries, and Diablo was always there and simultaneously not there at all. To top things off, Lena's training was all done outside of the school now too. She knew Astoria was the best place to learn what she was capable of, but finding her place within this community never seemed to get easier.

By the time she got home, her dad was gone and her mom was asleep. Lena imagined her mom hiding under their protective blanket and felt a pang of jealousy. Lena wanted nothing more than to slip away from reality too. Her phone buzzed.

It was Solei. "I'm sorry about how things happened today. Talk soon?"

Lena didn't respond. She knew Solei meant well, but it still hurt. They were the only ones who had the chance of seeing Diablo through

Lena's eyes. She expected that to mean more than what it evidently did.

A new message came in as she was closing her screen. It was from the group text. "Traps all set. Meet me at Ward A at 11:00 p.m. Lena, if you don't make him talk, we will." Attached was an image of holy water.

Furious, Lena instantly replied, "Don't do anything! I'll head there right now." It was only 7:00 p.m., but four hours still seemed like too short a time to talk Airess out of whatever nonsense was in her head. As Lena flew out the door, she swore she heard that soft whisper from Diablo once again. "Stay."

Lena's new title of trainee at Ward A made entering the ward much easier. She was grateful she didn't have to sneak in this time. Lena had already decided she wasn't calling her dad, but leaving a paper trail would only benefit her. When she arrived, she walked straight up to the front desk and asked how to check in. The lady there, Ipy, was more than happy to care for Lena as she walked her through the basic admin practices. When Lena asked how to get to Ina's room to meet with her mentor, Ipy was all the merrier to show her the way.

Airess hadn't mentioned where to meet up, or acknowledged Lena's early arrival, but an educated guess implied Ina's room was the best place to start. Lena knocked on the door. She watched the white sterile rectangle transform into an entryway out of a fairy tale. The entrance morphed to a large undefined shape with a rich wooden color. The ridges within the wood became extremely pronounced. Thick threads of ivy lined the sides of the coniferous masterpiece. Lena felt like she was an ant standing next to a redwood tree. The door creaked open.

"Hello?" Lena peered in.

"You're here early. I wonder why that is?" Airess was inside the room working on something in the corner.

"Airess, please. I only want to talk." Lena walked in and sat atop a gigantic mushroom.

"Lena, I'm not sure what you would like me to say. You've been a really good friend in the short time we've known each other, but there's a lot going on that you don't understand." She brought over a warm cup of liquid to Lena.

"I know I'm new, but I'd never protect anyone I thought was harmful or dangerous. I'm telling you, Diablo has a good heart; no matter who he comes from. If you'd only give him a chance, I'm positive you'd see it too."

"I don't need to hold your hand to know how much you believe that. Solei knows it too and, for what it's worth, Tao gave me a full-length lecture about using my powers on people without their consent. You're not alone. I know the things you say are what you strongly believe in, we all do."

"Then why do I feel like no matter how loud or continuously I scream, no one hears me?"

"Because we've had years of dealing with this world and know how it works. Here, ogres tend to be ogres, and demons.... Well, there's only one we know of and he's probably a demon, Lena."

"But what if he's not? What if he's not that at all?"

"Lena, I can completely understand how someone may not

want to be tied to their ancestry line, but Diablo has always embraced it. He has never once denied who his ancestors are. Plus, I mean, he has horns, Lena."

Lena was working hard to keep calm and control her anger. Diablo may never have denied the name they called him, but in her gut she knew those weren't horns. Dream or not, Lena knew they were the tips of a moon. "Is that how you felt about Kohl too?"

Airess' eyes became stern. "What do you mean? Kohl has nothing to do with this."

"You said you'd understand if someone hated their lineage. The first day I met Kohl he told me he hated his talents. He hated who he came from. Did you understand that with him?"

"I have done nothing but good for him! How dare you, Magdelena Basil!"

The door opened. "Looks like we arrived at the right time." Solei and Tao walked in. Airess gave them a confused look. "Lena said she was heading over in the group chat and we decided maybe we should too."

"Definitely that and not at all because we thought you two couldn't hold a civil conversation." Tao sat next to Lena, her mouth agape in protest.

"Easy, little cub. We came to help."

To help Airess. "I know. So what's the plan?" Lena tried to conceal her emotions as best she could.

"On second thought, I'm not so sure—" Airess tried to retract Lena's invitation but was briskly dismissed by Solei.

"You're sure you want to do this?" Solei offered. Lena accepted.

"Good, because without you, we've got nothing," Tao stated. Airess shot him a look. "Huh, I didn't think that was a big secret. Now I know."

"Ignore him. We have plenty. This is a good thing, Lena! I know you want to help; can't you see that's what we all want too? We can do this as a team! Then we'll get all of our belongings back and everyone can go into the portal safely. After that, we can forget about all this stuff. Right? Won't that be nice?" Airess was trying to be more amenable with the others around.

"Of course, I'd love to get past all this. It seems easier said than done though." Lena had mixed feelings.

"I can't even imagine what this all feels like to you right now, but you've got us!" Airess grabbed her hands then dropped them immediately. "Oops! Sorry! See? I'm learning too." The healer blushed a little as giggles emerged amongst the group. "Ready to hear what I've learned?" Everyone nodded.

"Diablo comes to Ward A almost nightly. He tends to check in after dark and leaves before daylight, go figure. When I looked through the sign-in books to see who he visits, it wasn't legible. I know he's obsessed with angels solely being trained for the portals, so I tried to find other angels that are residents here, besides Ina, obviously. Only two came up in all my searches. Turns out angels aren't very common here. Their rooms aren't particularly close to one another, but I was able to find a route that connects them. My guess is Diablo took all the stolen items to one of them for guidance. There are four vantage points along my route that give us clear views to catch him. If each of us takes a spot, we can alert the others once we find him. Together, we can surround him and make him confess."

"Make him confess? I thought the whole point of this was to get our gear back?" Lena disliked every part of Airess' plan.

"Right, same thing." Airess disregarded her. "When he confesses, we can grab the magical items and turn him in to Principal Chromwell."

"P.C.? Why? He's not even a student?" Tao was questioning Airess' strategy now too.

"Whatever, I'll pick someone else." Airess sighed in frustration. "All I need to know is are you in or are you out?"

"Lena, are you able to use your sight to see or sense Diablo's presence?" Tao asked.

"I don't know. I've tried repeatedly, but the few times I've seen him have tended to be because he wanted me to. I'm not sure my talent has had anything to do with it." Defeat was heavy in Lena's voice. "I need to know he's going to be okay if we catch him. I don't want anything bad to happen to him."

"We're not here to hurt anyone, Lena," Solei confirmed authoritatively.

Airess shrugged. "He'd deserve it."

"Why do you hate him so much? What has he ever done to you?" Lena's voice came out more as a shout than she intended.

"We don't have time to work out your feelings for a devil, Lena."

Solei flinched. "Airess, Diablo's possible bloodline to the devil doesn't inherently make him evil." Their voice carried an edge to it.

"Honestly, sometimes I have the same thoughts too, Airess. I'm no fan of Lucifer, but Diablo doesn't come around often enough to see him as this huge threat," Tao remarked.

"Tell that to Kohl, Tao. He was already lost to begin with. Then he met up with Diablo and now he's powerless. Additionally, all of our protection for our covert operation is missing. Meaning, in a way, now we're all powerless too. See the trend? Do you want the same fate, Tao Vovi?"

"Kohl lost his powers due to his own choices, Airess." Lena tried to comfort her, but Airess pulled away.

"Choices that involve you and our person in question. He had no idea saving you would pull his magic from him. Even by Diablo's standards, Kohl had no reason being in that portal."

"None of us did." Lena tried to sympathize.

"Kohl's preferences have always been different from ours, Airess. We won't end up like him," consoled Solei.

"You're right, we won't. I'm making sure of it." Airess stood up and passed out three copies of a scribbled map. "These are our four stations. I'll be closest to the entrance of Ward A. That's the far right point. Then Solei, then Lena, then Tao. I'll walk everyone to their post. Make sure your phones are out and working so we can communicate. Text if you see Diablo or anything else suspicious." She glared at Lena.

"That's enough, Airess; time to go." Solei took the lead out the door.

Chapter 11
Tricks and Traps

Each member of the group had a station they were assigned to. Airess was perched perpendicular to the main entrance and the meditative gardens. Down that hallway was Solei at an architecture desk filled with loads of blueprints. Within their direct line of sight was Lena located in a small reading nook.

Lena suspected she was supposed to be closer to the edge of the nook in order to see Tao at

his designated chess table.
However, she took the opportunity
to find comfort in her surroundings.
The nook was filled with rugs,
couches, pillows, and piles of books
scattered about. The walls were
dark and absorbed the ambient
light from the halls. Lena found a
large blanket and wrapped herself
up in it. She curled up on one of the
nearby couches. Hours passed with
nothing, not even texts from Airess.
That was the highlight of this
endeavor. Lena couldn't understand
why Airess had such a negative
impression of Diablo. He was
caring, protective. Lena felt a pang
of guilt. She knew she needed to be
here to hear the details of the trap,
but she was hesitant to follow
through with it. Debating between

sabotaging her friends' efforts and capturing Diablo made her stomach feel sick. She didn't want to do either, but letting Airess near Diablo, without at least trying to intervene, was incomprehensible. With the picture of the holy water at the front of Lena's mind, she had no idea what Airess was capable of.

Lena rolled over onto her back and discovered she could see the moon. She hadn't noticed before, but the back wall was transparent. She counted stars to pass the time. A knock startled her. She searched but couldn't see anyone. She sat up and heard a book fall down. She picked it up and read where it had been bookmarked:

"For what you see and hear depends a good deal on where you are standing: it also depends on what sort of person you are."

Lena closed the book. She glanced at the title. *The Magician's Nephew* by C. S. Lewis.

"Subtle," she chided.

"Right?" She could hear the pride in Diablo's voice.

Lena used her gift. She could barely make out a faint glimmer in the moonlight. "You plan on coming inside anytime soon or...?"

"You plan on capturing me anytime soon or...?"

How did he know? "I...." She paused. *Is he laughing at me?*

"Just so you know, you'd be the worst kidnapper ever."

"Thanks?" Lena grabbed her stomach; the thought of seeing Diablo again was not easing her nerves.

"Oh, calm down." He stepped into the nook from the back wall.

Lena tapped the window; it was solid as glass. She inspected Diablo curiously. Then she remembered Solei.

"Get down!" she begged. He didn't seem to care but obeyed anyway.

"I'm not scared of your friends, Lena. I've faced a lot worse."

"Fine, but I am!"

He chuckled again. "You're something else, you know that?"

"Shh!" Lena could see Solei glancing over to the commotion they were making. She pretended to read the book she'd picked up earlier. She was holding it upside down.

"Lena Basil going rogue, who could've guessed it?" Diablo mocked.

"I'm not going rogue!"

"Oh? Is hiding me from view part of the trap?"

"How do you know about that anyway?"

"Easy, Airess hates me."

"I can't deny that, but how does that imply a trap?"

"When people hate a demon, creativity isn't their strong suit."

Lena couldn't suppress her laughter. "Airess is kind of obsessed with you." She peered over the couch at him.

"Most people are." Diablo winked at her.

"I can't even." Lena turned, hiding her smile and blushing cheeks.

He sat up a little higher. "What's your next move, Basil?"

Next move ... with you?

"It doesn't look like you're trying to trap me, but you're clearly on a stakeout. Why are you here, Lena?"

She scrambled for a moment. Unsure of what to say, she blurted out her first coherent thought. "You were mad at me."

"You're here because I was mad at you?"

Lena nodded and then shook her head.

"That clears that up then."

Lena scrunched up her face. She was flustered. "I had a dream. A couple dreams, I guess." She averted her eyes. "They're usually fantastic, but the last one ended horribly. We got into a terrible fight. You were absolutely furious with me. I couldn't stand that being the last time I saw you." She spoke the end of her statement so softly it was barely audible.

Diablo was speechless for a moment. "Whatever happened, everything's all right now." He put his hand over hers. "I promise."

Lena was relieved and anxious all at once. He was holding her hand, in real life! "If you knew we laid a trap for you, why did you come?"

"Curiosity killed the cat?" He raised his eyebrows.

"That's an awful expression and an even worse reason."

He smirked. "I have worse reasons, want to hear them?"

Lena's phone dinged. It was Solei. "Airess is walking over. Be more discreet." Her jaw dropped.

Diablo leaned over to see the message. "Time's up! See you, Lena." He stood up, hiding his face in the hood of his jacket. His backpack snagged on an old staple in the couch.

"I'll help!" Lena jumped to tug his backpack. It ripped immediately. All of the lost magical items spilled out onto the floor. She fell back in shock. She could hear footsteps running towards them.

Diablo dropped the bag, ready to run. He muttered a single response before disappearing into the night. "Whatever you do, Lena, don't trust anyone."

~~~~~~~~~~~~~~~~~~~~~~~~~~~~~~

Lena's head was spinning. She had been mute for days. Of course, Airess had plenty of answers to offer. Her ego and pride were at an all-time high after that mess in the reading nook. The healer could not stop talking about it. It made Lena sick. Even Tao and Solei tried to redirect their conversations to other topics. Training for the portal was the only time Lena was willing to be around everyone. She threw herself into practicing. The less time she had to think, the more time she had to trust her instincts. Lena couldn't explain why she was clinging to Diablo's last words so hard, but she was. She was going to trust herself above everyone else.

Solei had tried to talk a few times, probably about Diablo, but Lena evaded them.

Lena actually became quite good at evading in general. She'd often overhear the adults talking about her progress. No one could hit her on the training field, even when they tried to. She always felt she knew what was coming next and then simply avoided it. When she focused solely on her opponent, evasion was even easier. As long as her mind was calm, her body was moving before her senses had the time to process. What Lena wouldn't give for those superhuman reflexes in other parts of her life. Where was this talent a few nights ago?

Her increased trust in herself was undeniably showing benefits, but Lena still wanted more. There was only one more sleep until the quintet entered the portal. She wondered if the rest of the team felt as fragmented as she did. Airess, of course, seemed to be glowing every step of the way, but Lena wondered how much of it was a show. Solei remained steady. They were forever strong, forever brave; a constant among chaos. It hurt Lena to be pulling away from them. The bond they shared with Lena in the mist was like nothing else she had ever felt before. She felt whole and empowered being connected to Solei. Not to mention the moment atop the electrical tower, when Solei showed their vulnerability for the first time. Lena could still feel anger in her chest thinking of their former bullies. It seemed confusing to her now why Airess and Solei were so close. At first, Lena had desperately wanted the three of them to grow inseparable. Those first days were so intense. Things had changed too fast.

"Lena!" It was Tao. "You were incredible out there! Did you even use your shield today? Where did you learn how to dodge like that?"

She hadn't used her shield once today. Not wanting to come off arrogant, she downplayed her success. Tao kept waiting. A shrug was clearly not going to be an acceptable answer. "I feel it, I guess.

My opponent's movements, their actions. My body just knows."

"Wow. I've never seen Solei work so hard to take someone down before. I thought their lacrosse playing was intense, but today was next level!" He sat down next to Lena.

Lena hadn't noticed. She smiled being at the same level as Solei. "Not bad for a newbie then?"

Tao's face lost its playfulness. "Lena, I don't think we can call you that anymore." He nudged her. "You're truly incredible out there. I know the professors we have in this group aren't rooted in strategic combat, but I don't think it'd matter."

Lena chuckled. "You don't like talking about it, but I'm sure you'd see me coming. I can't imagine getting past the almighty Tao Vovi."

"I've already failed at that." There was an awkward silence. "I know things aren't great right now, but the team's getting together to celebrate tonight. You should come. I can't promise it won't end poorly, but most of us would like to be together."

Lena cringed. "I don't know, Tao...."

"I didn't need a premonition to see that answer coming."

"Hey, since you're here, can I ask something?"

"You can always ask; it's my answer that's debatable."

Lena rolled her eyes, sometimes he was so Tao. "Do you think everything went south because of Diablo?"

She watched him flinch with annoyance. "I can't answer that, Lena."

"Because you don't know?"

"Because I'm in an impossible situation. I can't get any more involved in this. I've already overstepped."

"What? Didn't you just ask me to go out with you all tonight?"

"Yes, Lena, but that was different."

"Enlighten me then. How is me asking your opinion getting you overly involved when you, not two sentences before, asked me to essentially walk into a bear trap?" Lena's cheeks were hot with anger.

Tao put his hands up in the air to signify his surrender. "You're right. I shouldn't have come over. I'm sorry, Lena. Good luck tomorrow. I genuinely wish you the best." He left.

Lena threw herself back onto the plush grass. *Why do things always end like this?* That was clearly not how she wanted that to go. She only wanted a friend; someone she could actually talk to about everything. Lena was tired of having to carry it all alone. She was exhausted. Time to put her walls back up. She wasn't going to leave herself exposed again. Vulnerability could wait until after the portal. As she got up to leave, she saw Solei waiting for her. Lena took a deep breath and bolted the opposite way. Whatever they had been trying to say could wait until another day. Lena wasn't going to have another interaction like she'd had with Tao today. She was done.

~~~~~~~~~~~~~~~~~~~~~~~~~~~~~

The team was dressed in full gear when Lena arrived to the portal the next morning. Rubber boots, rain jackets, hats, goggles, and, of course, their token magical item. Lena kept the shield with her.

Despite everything, she had grown exceedingly accustomed to it.

"Principal Chromwell should be arriving in about fifteen minutes; then we will be on to our scheduled departure," Doctor Palaios announced.

"You ready, Magpie?" Lena's dad was nervous. He had already twisted one water bottle completely in half and the second one wasn't looking like it had too much longer to go.

Lena rubbed his arm. "I'm fine, Dad. You know all the hard work the team has put into this, and that includes everyone, not just the five going in. Professor Vontari and Tao have studied Indra relentlessly, you and Solei have put so much thought into what items will protect us best, and the rest of us have been on the field every day. Things are a lot different now than the first time I went in. We're basically The Avenging Angels 2.0."

Kasim gave his daughter a weak smile. "That's what I'm worried about, my love."

Lena went to say something, though she had no idea what, but luckily Solei interrupted. Kasim was needed elsewhere, giving Lena a reprieve. She sat against the wall, ready to escape to her music, when Tao came over and lightly kicked the sole of her boot.

Lena put down her ear buds. "Back for more already? I thought I had bought myself a solid week of avoidance strategies with our last conversation."

Tao didn't react. "Be careful today."

"I will." Lena paused for him to say something more. He didn't. "Thanks."

Tao stalked out. Lena was debating trying to process what had happened when Airess came over. *Oh joy.*

"Lena." Airess spoke pompously.

"Airess." Lena responded skeptically.

"I've come to tell you the plan."

Lena gestured for the healer to continue.

"The two professors will be our information hubs. Between Professor Vontari's knowledge of Indra and Doctor Palaios' historical background, no question should be left unanswered. Solei, of course, will be our primary offense while I will keep everything running smoothly. You will then be our first line of defense and our scout. If you see anything out of the ordinary you need to let all of us know immediately, especially me," she emphasized with pursed lips. "After all, seeing the worst does seem to be your speciality."

Ah, there is it. Lena had known Airess would slip in a jab somewhere. "I'm fairly confident that's what we've spent all week doing, but thanks anyway. You're involved as always."

"I hope one day you'll see that I only want what's best, Lena. I had hoped that, with your powers, that would've been rather visible."

"You're not the only one who was disappointed with what I saw once I found my way past the veil."

Airess opened her mouth to respond, but Principal Chromwell commanded the room's attention. She was dressed as if she was attending a grand ball from the medieval period. Her robe was lavish and outstretched. While it seemed fitted to her core, the sleeves and skirt billowed out into the room. The contrast between the heavy crushed velvet and light flowing chiffon made a striking visual impact.

"My strongest. My bravest. My heroes. We gather here this morning not for battle but for peace, with hopes of inclusion, diversity, and preservation beating in the core of our hearts. We aim not to condemn but to protect for evermore. You have been chosen. You will fulfill our task, for, if not, then we may all become victims of history ourselves. A possibility too grave for pure hearts. I wish you all perseverance in your haste and monumental success that Legacy Academy has not been able to obtain for decades. Please, make yourselves proud out there today.

Your best will always be good enough." With that, P.C. departed.

"Assume your positions, squad," Solei commanded.

"On the count of three," Doctor Palaios declared.

"Wait!" It was Tao. "Shouldn't there be some sort of battle cry or something?" He was freaking out.

"I once heard of someone praying, 'Anything but seaweed!'" Solei playfully bumped Lena.

OMG. That was me. I had completely forgotten people could shapeshift when jumping into the portal. Why did no one cover that in training?!

"Anything but seaweed!" The group had already counted and

were taking their leap of faith into the realm before them. Solei grabbed Lena's hand and yanked her hard to keep her caught up. The slight sting of their touch pulled Lena back to reality just in time.

She intentionally waited to open her eyes once she felt the wave of magic pass over her. She tried to move her body. So far, everything felt normal. She opened one eye and wiggled what she hoped was her hand out in front of her. Win. It was a hand. She could see a leg too and a foot. Taking it all in, Lena found herself kneeling on a cloud. Standing, she braced herself for harsh winds, flooding rains, and raging storms. The fluffy white cloud shifted underneath, keeping Lena's balance stable. *What?*

She gazed off into the distance. Her sight felt razor sharp. The sky was a vibrant blue. The land, if you could even call it that, was comprised of soft white clouds that frequently readjusted to the walkers' benefit. This realm was heaven. Even the air smelled sweet. The only unsettling aspect was that it appeared uninhabited. There was no sign of existence as far as Lena could see. She decided to cautiously wander forward. The base of her palm stung again; she checked for injury. There was a bug, an electrical bug. Solei had given Lena another mental implant.

Lena couldn't deny how incredibly useful using this could be, especially considering her current isolation, but there were too many complications last time. She groaned, tapping the little device. Diablo's words echoed in her mind. "Don't trust anyone." Lena put the bug in her chest pocket and trekked on through the clouds.

She had been walking a while when she finally saw a warm glow off in the horizon. Despite the distance traveled, Lena felt no strain in her legs. She felt no exertion at all. She pressed on towards the light. Towers of gold started to form. They were blindingly bright and emanated heat. The clouds below her feet began to form the shapes of stairs; a fruity aroma intensified as she climbed. A speck off in the distance seemed to be moving towards the comforting columns. Lena rushed after the small dot. Without the feeling of exertion, her pace was impeccable. She recognized the speck; it was Professor Vontari. He was moving at mach speed towards the room beyond the golden structures. Lena yelled, straining to get his attention. She was pretty sure he could hear her, but she couldn't break his concentration. Worrying what spell or condition he might be under, Lena debated following him. A voice made her reconsider.

"Lena! LENA!" It was Solei.

Stress that Lena didn't even know she had lifted off her shoulders.

"You're okay?" Solei examined Lena's face and arms to verify that she was indeed real.

"Yeah, you?"

"Yeah, I'm surprisingly good. Never better even. I feel supercharged."

"Same. That's weird though, right? I shouldn't feel this good?"

"Not at all. This is nothing like what we were told."

"I saw Professor Vontari. He seemed off."

"Me too. I was tracking him for a while. I didn't land near anyone, but I caught the feeling of his energy. He was practically buzzing."

"Oh, speaking of buzzing, I found this." Lena pulled out the implant.

Solei reddened. "I didn't want anything to happen to you. Not that I think you're not capable—"

"I understand. It's fine." Seeing her friend's compassion, Lena slipped the bug into her ear. They both winced. Lena looked at her friend and mentally asked, *Good?*

Solei's smile brimmed ear to ear. *I made some changes too.*

Flashbacks to Solei in Ward B flooded Lena's mind.

Yup, that would be the reason for the changes. You didn't think I'd repeat all that did you?

Lena hadn't thought at all.

"Don't doubt yourself, Lena. You're capable of more than you get credit for. I've seen that."

Lena waited for an insult to follow, but it never did. She studied the gargantuan structure up ahead. "Do you have any idea what that is?"

"Probably something godly?"

Lena started laughing far harder than she should've. "Should we go in?"

Up the stairs they ascended, the structure's radiance magnifying with each step. When the heat started to burn too strongly, and Lena was ready to ask Solei to turn back, the discomfort stopped. One foot past the columns and all was resolved. The chamber within the towers showed no end. The new floor gleamed a shiny whitish silver. Intricate carvings divided the boundless area into sections. Detailed drawings and paintings hung freely in the air, each one ornate; each delicate and precious. Lena was shocked. She had never seen such wealth. She inclined toward Solei to share her astonishment, but they were crouched near the ground.

"Part of this is white gold. Not all of it. Some of these materials I've never encountered, but there are definitely elements of a conductor here."

Lena felt silly being so far off task. She tapped her foot on the ground. "Definitely." Solei gave her a side eye. Professor Vontari's voice began echoing in their chamber. They walked in on him praying ... to Indra.

"Hey devo ke dev! Ye ahankaari manushya aap ko swarg se hatane aaye hai. Ye kisi asuro se kam nahi hai, prabhu. Mujh jaisa manushya aap ko dandvat pranam karta hai."

Oh, Lord of the Lords! These egotistical men have come to remove you from heaven. They are no less than Asuras, Lord. A man like me bows to you. Lena's mind briskly deciphered his speech.

What's an Asura? Solei asked.

It's kind of like a demigod or a demon, it depends on context. Lena tried to explain. Solei's eyes went wide.

Professor Vontari kneeled upon an elevated platform in the center of a circle; he bowed before a large chair. His body lay flat and his hands were outstretched with an object Lena couldn't make out. He was kissing the ground between words. Lena and Solei stood there watching in confusion and betrayal. Two other shapes, presumably Airess and Doctor Palaios, appeared along the perimeter, but no one moved. No one spoke. When the prayer was completed, Professor Vontari lay still, sobbing.

The wind made a sudden shift. The air's sweet aroma became sickeningly pungent; Lena felt the urge to gag.

Solei spoke first. "That smell is...."

Putrid. The word you're looking for is putrid, Lena answered inwardly, too scared to open her mouth.

Making eye contact, Solei agreed and plugged their nose.

"Nashwar! Swarga mein! In kshudra manushyo ki yahan aane ki himmat kaise hui! Nikal jao tum sab yahan se abhi ke abhi!"

Mortal! In heaven! How dare the petty humans come here! Get out of here all of you, now!

410

"That's not good. RUN!" Lena shouted; Solei was already on their feet. Both of them motioned Airess and Doctor Palaios to follow. They ran as fast as they could out of the golden edifice. The once fluffy white clouds were now turning a damp and swampy grey. A monsoon quickly descended upon them. The resistance of the ground was rapidly increasing as well. It felt like they were trudging through a foot of thick mud.

"We are." Solei lifted up their mud-caked hands as proof. "If we don't find the others soon, Lena, I'm not sure we'll be able to. Not in any strategic way at least."

"Cover me. I'll see what I can do." Lena closed her eyes and concentrated. All her regular senses proved useless. Being human had no benefit here. She peered into the abyss with her sight. Whatever benefits she had earlier were gone. There was a small flicker. It wasn't identifiable, but Lena was certain it existed. An answer, in Solei's voice, came from within. *It's our best shot.*

The rubber boots were painfully heavy. Thunder rolled on above. Electric sparks started to appear before Lena's feet. Solei was hardening the ground for them.

"Step on the fulgurites," they instructed.

"What the heck is a fulgurite?!"

Solei sighed aloud in frustration. "The glassy rocks I'm creating. Come on!"

Lena did as she was told. Getting through the terrain became much easier. Off to the right, she spotted a rock jutting out from the ground. "This way!" she urged. Solei solidified the area shadowed by the rock and the two found shelter atop the warm glass. Solei was visibly exhausted.

Indra's voice exploded overhead. It hurt Lena's ears to hear.

"I didn't understand that one, Lena," Solei yelled.

In a scornful voice Lena recited, "Coming to renounce me from my throne, are you? You'll see what happens to those who oppose the God of gods!" A noise similar to a trumpet resounded.

Solei mouthed the word, "Elephant," to Lena. An image of the multi-headed mammal on the portal door came into Lena's mind. Was it a memory or did Solei put it there? Solei tapped Lena's shoulder then pointed to themself.

Lena could see the rain behind her friend lifting. They were on a riverbed of a wide, flowing, murky waterway. Barren plains were off to their left. Lena ran out into the clearing. She could feel Solei's anger, but she had to get a better view if she was going to be of any help. Her idea worked. She saw

Doctor Palaios lying on the ground a few meters away. *I'm faster,* entered Lena's thoughts.

Solei was gone before Lena could debate the idea. The noise in the dark swirling sky crescendoed. Lena watched the lacrosse star reach the professor and start back when a bolt shot before them. Maniacal laughter filled the skies. Indra was a cat playing with their prey and Solei was the mouse. Lena went to go help but was pulled back. She spun around, expecting to find Airess, but it was Diablo. Before a single thought could form, she ripped the bug out of her ear and wrapped her arms around him.

"It's not safe here, Lena. You need to go."

"But you're here too."

"Not because I want to be." Lena gave him a quizzical look; he pulled her hand to his heart. "Please go, Lena. This realm is draining my powers. I can't protect you here. Not completely. P.C. should never have agreed to this in the first place. Her ego got the best of her. She was too focused on vicariously reliving her glory days to listen to reason. I'll beg you if I need to."

"I'm not alone. Four others came with me." She recalled the incident with Professor Vontari. "There are at least three others that are stuck in the field. I can't find Airess."

"If I said I only cared about one single person here, and very much did not care about the rest, that wouldn't sway you would it?"

"Diablo...."

"I know. I know. I'm on it. I'll find the healer. She never tends to be far away from me anyway."

Lena smirked then presented Solei's implant to him. "This has been the only time I've trusted someone else since you told me not to."

He grinned. "If we make it out of this, I have another thing to tell you."

"That's so cheesy. You're supposed to be better than that."

"And yet...." Diablo kissed Lena's cheek and went off into the shadows.

Solei arrived shortly after. They were terribly out of breath. Doctor Palaios was groggy but conscious. "Lena, are you okay? I lost the signal with you!"

Lena's face was burning red. She was holding her cheek where Diablo's lips had just been. She wanted to explain but couldn't.

Solei reached across and put the bug back in. "I don't care about him anymore. You love him. Airess hates him. I can't be involved in that. What I am involved in is the need to bring you home in one piece. I also would like to come home in one piece and stay that way this time."

Lena wasn't positive, but she swore that, once the electrical connection was established again, Solei flushed at the flood of new emotions.

"I don't understand," Doctor Palaios muttered to herself. "It doesn't make sense. It doesn't make any sense."

An ominous roar sounded above them. The rains kept their distance, but the adjacent surroundings had grown notably darker.

Doctor Palaios crawled outside the covering to distinguish the sound. "AIRAVATA! The elephant!

They're going to crush us!" The team fled the scene. The students flanked their professor, who had no idea of where to go. The trio were sitting ducks with no protection. Solei instinctively resumed taking charge, steering the group outside the shadow of the impending elephant.

Airavata's size was monstrous. As they ran, Lena tried to use her sight to spot anything useful, but the only distinguishable shape was a flat foot ready to squish the threesome. There was no way out. They stood no chance. Lena flashed a mental image of a huddle to Solei while she launched to tackle them both and slammed her magical shield into the ground.

To say that the ground shook with the ferocity of an earthquake when Airavata landed would be an understatement. Lena held tightly on to her comrades as the force of the elephant's foot propelled them straight into the air. Their protective dome remained intact as they flew, but the shield's bottom was completely exposed. They all gaped in shock and horror as they were hurled up the godly creature's body. Their vision was obscured by thick clouds. Lightning danced around them in the sky, becoming more concentrated the higher they rose. For a brief moment, they could see what was potentially Indra. They saw a strong looking torso with an extended belly. At least two arms functioned on each side. Bejeweled garments faded in and out of sight, as did a gleaming club with a ribbed spherical head.

"That's his astra," Doctor Palaios exclaimed.

A voice boomed, once again speaking Hindi. Lena translated in sync. "Trespassers! How dare you think you humans could walk into Indraloka unannounced? Now you get to feel the wrath of the all mighty Lord Indra." With his last word, an unknown force vigorously started hurling them diagonally towards the ground. Concurrently, the outlines of Indra were closing in above them. They watched as his burly body raised his astra into the air and shot pure energy into the ground below. The dome bounced away from the astra's force as the team crashed into the newly created pit, their shield shattering around them. The depth of the astra's indentation was not nearly as immense as the formations protruding around it. They were less than ten feet below the surface, but the jagged piercing rock around them went well into the sky.

Solei immediately took the defensive. They drew their staff instinctively. Lena could feel a reprieve of Indra's energy through Solei. The rains were formidable. Without the cosmic elephant shielding them from the storm, the droplets hit hard and fast.

"We're not going to survive another strike like that! We're lucky enough that this one wasn't aimed at us!" Lena panicked.

"Indra's astra never misses. If this is where it made contact, then this is where Indra intended to smite." The professor rose to scout around.

"Solei." Lena tried to redirect her friend's attention. "Did you notice anything weird when we got closer to Indra?"

"Other than absolutely everything?"

Lena groaned. "Yes, other than absolutely everything."

"He puts out more energy than the entire city of Astoria. I've played with actual lightning bolts that felt like static compared to him.

Honestly, it's somewhat unbearable."

"I meant with his face. His face was changing so often I lost count of how many I saw. It was like there were multiple versions of him trapped in one body. I don't remember that from Professor Vontari's lessons. Do you?"

Solei shook their head. "No, but I'm not sure we can consider him a credible source of information any longer."

"Good point." Lena scanned the area for Doctor Palaios.

They were making their way back to the group, surprisingly, with Diablo. "I seem to have found the target for the attack."

"Diablo!" Lena raced to hug him. His clothes felt crispy.

"Can't kill the dead, huh Diablo?" Solei glanced over in between shifting their guarding positions.

"Fun fact, the devil isn't actually dead. I expect you already knew that though." Diablo turned into ... nothing. He vanished right out of Lena's arms. "Hard to kill a shadow though." He materialized right back to where he was, looking directly at Lena.

Not knowing what to say, Lena apprehensively responded, "Did you find Airess?"

"About that." He opened up his backpack. "I can't be certain, but I'm like ninety-nine percent sure she's right here."

Everyone but Diablo was frozen. In his hand, he held a small potted plant with a bubble gum pink base.

Chapter 12
Rage and Remorse

Diablo was right. Airess was a plant. Doctor Palaios accepted the news forthwith, but Lena and Solei needed more time. Solei actively challenged Diablo. Calm as ever, he walked over to them and pretended to drop the bubble gum pot. Solei caught the small seedling without a second thought. The whole group watched as the plant's flimsy stems leaned towards Solei's chest and began to thicken.

"If my botany background holds true, this little Dypsis will grow into an areca palm."

"That's good, isn't it?" Lena asked. "That's the counterpart to the ring Solei demonstrated."

"It's supposed to help you breathe underwater—" Solei eyed the water level rising in their pit "— which might become extremely relevant sooner rather than later."

"All of that is true, but this plant is in the Arecaceae family. That means their growth, and survival, is based on tropical and subtropical climates. Your friend needs heat and light in order to survive." Doctor Palaios tried to deliver the news gently.

Lena knew she wasn't the only one noticing the contrast between that information and the gloomy skies with chilled raindrops that enveloped them all. Solei pulled a necklace out from underneath their thick coat. They squeezed it tightly for a moment and when they let go, it glowed like a star. The orb around Solei's neck helped pierce through the darkness. Airess' newly sprouted leaves curled around it, forming a tiny heart.

"Even more of a reason for us to get out of here then." Solei embraced their flora-based friend. "I'm not letting anything happen to any of you. I say we abandon the mission and retreat home.

Professor, do you know how to get us out of here?"

Doctor Palaios' face went pale. "I ... I don't know. Why don't I know?"

"Getting into portals is the easy part. Getting out, well, you're going to need a god for that," Diablo explained. "Also, to answer your question, Professor, I think this realm subdues whatever god-given gifts we possess. I imagine the longer we're here the more human we'll become."

A low roar growled above them. "ASURAS!"

"That isn't a compliment he's bellowing. There's no way Indra agrees to us leaving," Lena asserted.

"How about we change his mind then?" Diablo spoke confidently.

"And how do you propose we do that? We don't exactly have the upper hand here." The water around Solei was up to their torso. Their feet were slowly lifting off the ground. All four members of the group were starting to tread water.

Trying to diffuse any tensions, Lena chimed in. "If we want to sway his opinion, we need to come up with something he wants. Does anyone remember what Indra likes?"

Doctor Palaios seemed overly eager to finally have a helpful answer. "Wine! No. Mead! No. Soma! Yes, that's it! Soma!"

"Not that we have any, but I'm pretty sure Indra has a hefty supply of all of those. I'm still trying to get the smell of spoiled fruit out of my nose." Diablo cringed.

Doctor Palaios was back at it. "Indra defeated the great evil who obstructed the humans' prosperity and happiness. Humans were important to him once. He brought back the rains and sunshine to mankind as a gift."

Lena's head bobbed underwater; Diablo and Solei simultaneously reached to lift her up. Their surprise in each other's reaction didn't go unnoticed by Lena. "Not to be difficult, Professor, but Indra has a slightly different temperament today." Another bob under, another joint lift up.

Noticing they were about two feet from the top of the astra's crater, Solei tucked Airess into their jacket and secured her in place with a belt. They were ready to start climbing out. The crashing of the raging waters dominated over all other sounds. Diablo swam over to them. The two looked to be arguing, but Lena could only feel Solei's emotions. They were strong and adamantly against whatever they were being told. Then there was relief. Diablo came over to Lena and the professor, putting something small in their hands. He gestured for them to eat it.

Those are from Airess. She gave up some of her leaves; it won't be a perfect solution to the floods out there, but it'll be better than nothing, Solei calmly transmitted to Lena.

When the water brimmed the pit's opening, they could see that the lands had turned into a rushing river. Solei directed the four to lock their arms together; the chain formed a singular unit as the water carried them away. Every raindrop struck like a shard of ice. Solei was sending continuous positive vibes through their tether to Lena; Lena clutched on to them dearly, being mindful not to let her fears overpower the encouragement. The glow from Solei's pendant was frequently the sole visible light.

Diablo noticed erratic lines extending outside Solei's shadow. A weave of palm leaves were flailing in the current. He scrambled past the others in their formation, latching to the end of the freshly woven square. Tightening his grip on Airess' design, and using the water's force to his advantage, he dropped underwater to catch the group within the palm's loose netting. Airess' powers kept progressing. She was forming a carefully crafted canoe around her team. Solei was at the front of the makeshift boat, ready to steer.

Discreetly, they mouthed, "Thank you."

Indra called from above, "You! What are you doing alive? Vajra never misses!" The realm shook with the God of gods' every word.

"That's my cue!" Diablo pushed apart the vines of the watercraft. What was shaped as a canoe not a few minutes before was now becoming spherical. He planned his timing and dove straight into the frigid water.

"No!" Lena threw herself to stop him, but Airess' tendrils caught her and brought her back to safety.

"He knows what he's doing, Lena." Solei tried to comfort her, but their attention was split while navigating the vessel through the floods.

A fiery beam shone a few meters away, illuminating the dark sky. Indra went berserk. Instantly, the elephant and the god were charging towards the blazing ray. The beam turned off and appeared in another direction. The astra went in full swing towards it, creating more gouges and pillars across the land. Lena knew the astra couldn't miss, but as soon as the illumination attracted Indra's anger, it vanished into the pitch-black surroundings. *Into the shadows,* Solei corrected.

Oh my gosh! It was a diversion!

Lena wanted more information from Solei, but they had steered the team onto a riverbank. Solei needed a plan, now. "With Indra distracted, the river is manageable for the moment. We have some time to think, but Diablo can't keep at this for long. Indra's way too strong for him to keep risking his life like he is."

Lena turned towards the uproar behind her. She wanted to use her sight to decipher the faces she saw within Indra earlier. He was farther away than Lena would've liked, but from what she could tell, there were three overlapping images that were distinguishable. Within those images, though, there was more fast-paced imagery. The rapid changes caused a splintering pain in

Lena's mind; she had to take a break. Solei spoke for her.

"Professor, why is Lena seeing so many versions of Indra with her sight?"

"I suppose it's possible she's seeing him through the multiple depictions he has had through the years."

"Do you mean his different personas from the Vedas?"

"Oh no! Not just the Vedas, my young scholar, those mostly pertain to Hinduism. I mean who he is to his people in all the religions he makes appearances in. Indra is king in the Vedic religion, Hinduism, Buddhism, Jainism, Cham—"

"What?!" Solei was so mad they radiated energy. "We weren't taught any of that!"

"That kind of information would've been far too overwhelming for you all." There was a hint of condescension in the professor's tone.

"But the strong likelihood of dying isn't?" Solei's indignation was amplifying rapidly.

Doctor Palaios went to speak then decided against it. The heat emitting from Solei was increasing exponentially. Airess' leaves tried to absorb what heat they could, but Solei was livid. Lena hadn't seen Solei like this since their time in Ward B. The emotions they were projecting were full of rage. In desperation, Lena grabbed two large handfuls of mud and threw them at the largest surface of Solei's uncovered skin, their face. In the team's small circle, the world paused. No one dared to react, but the immediate cooling effect was evident. Solei wiped the wet dirt from their eyes. They spoke the next few words very slowly. "That is one solution."

"Is Indra forlorn in all of those religions?" Lena was attempting to take over for her friend. It was clear Doctor Palaios had the answer to their problem, but without the right questions they were just wasting time.

"I believe that is only the case in Hinduism and possibly in its precursor, the Vedic religion."

"Is he still worshiped in those other religions?" Solei was tracking exactly what Lena was thinking.

"Indra is the King of the Heavens! Of course he is worshiped. He's a revered leader of the gods. There's simply an unfavorable version of him that appears from time to time."

"If it's only sometimes, what's the catalyst?" Lena actively tried to hide her irritation.

"Almost always it is poor decision-making. Usually, that means a large consumption of soma, which is basically a godly liquor."

"Then this is something the other gods in his religion would've had to deal with?"

"Oh certainly! Two twin gods in Hinduism and a goddess of the same religion have an antidote for it."

"That would've been helpful to know when we were training, Professor." Solei's frustration was unmistakable.

Lena tried to deescalate the situation again. "What other things have helped the gods around him?"

There was a long pause. Doctor Palaios stood up, stepped out of the intricate ball of greenery, and told her pupils to stay put. Lena watched Solei. They were counting down from ten. Then Airess' sphere started noiselessly retracing the professor's steps until they were stopped at the base of a large formation.

Doctor Palaios had made her way atop the cliff adorned in an astonishing new set of clothes. Weakened, she could barely stand, but her appearance remained regal.

"Indra! I call upon the ruler of heaven, the King of Gods. I beg for your mercy and for your listening ear! Remember Govardhan. The insult from those mere mortals below you was similar then too. How dare they not worship you?

How dare they not give you offerings and uphold your puja!"

"Krishhhhhhnaaaaa." The way Indra said the word sounded like a deadly threat. Airavata trumpeted and trampled in the skies above them. The winds formed a vortex. Indra's astra was pointed directly at his new target—Doctor Palaios. She had the god's complete attention now, for better or worse.

Doctor Palaios forced herself upright, unwavering in the chaos around her. "Indeed. Krishna," she responded with a slight hiss. "Tell me, Lord Indra; tell me what happened to you. But please, I beg you, have pity on me and tell me your word in a way my mortal half can understand. For you, as you

currently are, are too great for me—
too strong, too brave, too godly for
my unworthy self to process."

Indra sneered at the mortal.
The eyes that covered his skin
glared. He looked deadly. With a
flick of his wrist, the elephant
traveled back to the clouds and
Indra stood before the professor.
His size had become human, but the
weight of his intimidation lingered.

"Lord Krishna, avatar of the
great Lord Vishnu, is a mighty
warrior. Only a fool would cast
doubt upon them," Indra taunted.

"Or yourself." Doctor Palaios
spoke stone faced, revealing no
emotion.

"Or myself." Indra circled around the professor, taking long slow strides. The golden charms jingled on his belt as he strode. "A god's only fault is when they forget their role as a god. We are the almighty. We are the rulers of heaven, of the sea, and all that lies in between. We maintain order and protect against the pandemonium that evil ensures. We are supreme for a reason, and thus, all our actions should demonstrate such greatness."

"As yours do, my lord." The professor fell before the god. A wince of pain escaped her mouth as she knelt at his feet.

Indra was appeased. In fact, all the Indras were. Lena had crept up the jagged rock early on in the conversation for a clearer view. "Why have you come before my throne today trespasser? Why have you come to play games and cast tricks in my domain?" Indra's voice was stern but smooth.

"We beg for your forgiveness, my Lord. I believe we may have been led here under false pretenses. We were sent to rescue you, but even the simplest of men can see that you do not need rescuing. You are as cunning and as swift as ever. You remain a righteous and godly king through and through."

"I am THE king. I will remain so for this eternity and all those subsequent to this." Indra stomped causing fissures to spider out into the ground from his foot. Lena held on to the crumbling rocks for dear life.

"Yes, my king," Doctor Palaios concurred.

"Even at my feet you lie, woman. Stand up and gather your friends. None of you deserve me. None of you smell like my children. I shall be done with you all soon. First, though, first you must all learn your lessons. Come, now!" The last two words emitted vibrations Lena could feel in her bones. She traversed the rocky ledge to stand beside her struggling teacher. As she prepared to hold Dr. Palaois steady, Diablo's shadows encircled her. Solei was quick to run to Lena's other side, complete with Airess in tow.

"Asuras, all of you, be gone and never come back. Dare you judge me, and my followers, whilst you root yourselves in treachery and deceit! I've suffered horrific punishments for crimes less severe than the band of you all have committed today. Out of sheer pity, I save you from curses, deformation, and lost dignity. Leave. Now. Never return or I'll be sure to let my brethren be the ones to find you." Indra waved his hand before the group and, just like that, all five travelers were laid out on Ward A's floor.

"Lena!" Both of her parents scooped her up immediately. They cried tears of joy as they held her. Lena looked to her other squad members. Airess, who was once again back to her human form, and Solei were holding on to each other, ensuring their mutual health. Tao was bunched up close to them, offering physical support when able. Doctor Palaios was standing, dusting herself off, appearing completely unscathed. Diablo, however, seemed to have sustained the worst damage. He was barely corporeal. The physicalities that were visible were deeply slashed and burned. The shade that represented him appeared unresponsive. Lena flung to his side. As she tried to whisper reassurances to the misty mass before her, she heard someone call out for a nurse. She refused to acknowledge the situation. She refused to let go. Vines crept in over her grip; looking up, she saw Airess.

"Trust me. I get it now." Airess offered her hands out to Lena as a peace offering. Solei stood next to the healer in agreement.

"As soon as we're cleared from medical, we can check on him too," Solei offered.

"Lena, let me stay with him for you." The friends turned towards Kasim. "I don't know what that is, but I'll keep an eye on it."

"Mhmm. Me too." Kamilah stepped forward proudly.

"Me three. You lot need to be examined by the academy's elite

crew of restorative staff. In
anticipation, we've added a few
specialists on hand. Nurse Galen
and I will help Miss Hikona and our
new friend here. Doctor Palaios,
and the rest of our fearless crew,
can find help ready and waiting at
the infirmary. When everyone is
back to proper shape, we can be
rejoined as one once again." There
was little to debate once Principal
Chromwell spoke. Nurse Galen,
Kasim, Kamilah, Airess, and Diablo
went in one direction with P.C. and
Doctor Palaios ushered Lena, Solei,
and the remaining attendants to
Ward B.

~~~~~~~~~~~~~~~~~~~~~~~~~~~~~~~

Lena put another "X" on her
calendar. She was counting down

the days until Diablo would wake up again, or, rather, when Selene would wake up again. That's what she accidently named him when her theory of his origin was proven right. Diablo wasn't a descendant of the devil at all but of a moon goddess. Airess had tried her best to treat him with her powers, but she couldn't keep him materialized. He literally kept slipping through her fingers. In a panic, she ran to harvest two incredibly scarce plants from Ward A that were strongly tied to the devil—dodder and deadly nightshade. She had hoped they would restore a physical balance within him. When Principal Chromwell walked in on Airess preparing to feed these to the poor boy, the principal could hold her silence no longer. P.C. stopped time itself to carefully dispose of the parasitic tendrils and deadly berries. Realizing she couldn't continue keeping his secret, Principal Chromwell called an emergency midnight meeting for those tending to Diablo's care. Lena sat in the dark room while P.C. explained a heartfelt story of love and despair.

"Many moons ago, there was a charming demi-goddess of the night. Her skin shone with the intensity of the sun, but her light was as gentle as fresh fallen snow. The village she was born into cherished the sweet girl at first glance, but murmurs quickly arose of the gods' wild jealousy towards her beauty. Her parents took her to

a local temple to establish peace,
but the child was instead met with
a curse on the first day of her birth.
The gods decreed that the child
could only be seen during the dark
hours and her pure white skin
would simply be a reflector of the
great sun her village worshiped.
When that immaculate central star
shone down upon the land, she
would be invisible outside of the
shadows. Embarrassed by her
translucent skin, she shied away
from other kids as they frolicked
and played in the daylight. Instead,
the girl would wait until moonlit
hours to be active and played alone
along her village's shoreline while
the rest of her community slept. The
humans around her deemed such
actions suspicious. They decreed

only evil had that much energy at night. They threatened to cast out her family from their coterie, slandering them as witches, imps, and demons. Heartbroken that her existence caused her parents so much pain, she fled at first chance; never to be seen again. The rumor was that our brave demi-goddess found shelter in a seaside cave not so far away from her former home. The villagers would sometimes see two brilliant white horses taking residence on a remote cliff and the glow of a fire deep within it. These stories lasted for decades. Folktales of all sorts raved about the White Witch of the Night."

Principal Chromwell lost herself in thought for a moment.

"That is how I first came to know of her. I was part of a scouting mission back then. In those times, anyone who came across as unusual, even if the uniqueness proved valuable, tended to be killed shortly after. Most Legacies and Descendants tried to lie low back then, but magic can only be repressed for so long without an explosion! I was determined to come bring the White Witch home to Legacy Academy, to show her what a life of acceptance could be like. Fate had a different plan though, divine or otherwise. You see, when I started near the mountain, I was overcome with a profuse sense of fear. Unsure if it was some sort of spell, or actual intuition, I pushed forward. My first discovery was the sound of a woman in tears and the faint cry of a baby. I ran straight up that slope into the warm cavern. She gauged my presence for what felt like eternity. I could tell she was frightened initially, but those feelings swiftly resolved into confusion. Cast in the moonlight, her skin sparkled like diamonds. You know, to this day, I have never seen a more ethereal sight. She walked towards me, whispered, 'Thank you,' and went out like a flame. I was left in a cold, dark, damp cave with a newfound baby in my arms." Principal Chromwell smoothed Diablo's haze. "I've been watching him from afar ever since."

Lena joined her unconscious beau to console him, caressing his sporadically materializing hand. "My Selene."

The name took like wildfire. Lena didn't mean to rename him; she didn't even really mean to say what she did out loud. Often her thoughts would race, scrutinizing over if he'd be mad at her when he came back. The results were always the same either way. Mad or not, seeing him whole and conscious was all that mattered.

Lena had been waiting for almost two weeks for any signs of improvement. Early on, Principal Chromwell had called in an expert to help Airess bring Selene back. Despite Airess' best efforts, helping Selene often caused her to faint. Professor Nakshatra was prompt in starting her analysis. She informed those who visited that treatments lasted from a new moon to a full moon. That meant one more day. Lena only had to hold out hope and keep her patience for one more day.

Thankfully, her friends had been remarkable. Solei, Tao, and even Airess couldn't deny the intent of Selene's actions in the portal. Selene had saved Airess, prioritized protecting Lena, and risked his own life without hesitation. All for the others to have a chance at getting back home. *Though I'm sure learning he wasn't a devil didn't hurt that transformation*, Lena mused.

Her phone dinged. There was a group text message from Solei.

Lena rolled over to open it. "I need you guys at Ward B. It's Airess. She fainted again, only this time she isn't waking up. She hasn't responded to any of Nurse Galen's treatments." Lena's sneakers were already on by the time Solei sent their second message. "I'm scared."

Lena didn't even take the time to respond, she just ran. Upon arriving at Legacy's campus, she bumped into Professor Nakshatra straight away.

"Lena! I'm glad to see you! I was going to try to call you."

"About Airess? Solei messaged me; I came as soon as I heard."

The teacher looked puzzled. "Airess? No dear, I wanted to talk to you about Selene."

"Selene?" Lena's heart was in her throat. She couldn't take any more bad news.

"Yes. Now, he isn't fully materialized yet, but it's coming along wonderfully! In fact, his vocal chords are clearly in full working order because he's called out for you by name frequently this morning."

My Selene. He's calling out for me. Lena had no idea what to do. She wanted to rush to Airess to make sure the healer was safe, and stand by the others if Airess wasn't, but ... Selene.

"Is he okay, Professor?"

"I think he will be by the full moon tonight!"

Lena looked at her watch, 4:00 p.m. "How many hours away is that?"

"Probably less than twelve. I must say, I thought you'd be more excited. You've been by his side nonstop."

"I am." *I so am!* "It's just that a friend of mine doesn't seem to be doing well and now I'm not sure what to do."

"Ah, I see. I have a solution. Why don't you come with me momentarily? If Selene's ears appear formed, you can reassure him of your presence. After that, you can skedaddle on over to your other friend. How does that sound?"

Relieved to have someone else handle her problem, Lena agreed. The walk was short, likely because of Lena's impatience. Principal Chromwell had decided to establish Diablo's care in Ward A and as much as the ward's labyrinth had troubled Lena in the past, it was becoming second nature to her now. In fact, she was so comfortable with the maze of Ward A it was hard not to run ahead of the visiting professor.

Lena tried to be careful entering the room. Everything was the same as when she had left it. A navy-blue darkness made the walls look like a perfect nighttime sky.

Small reflections of light acted as stars. Diablo lay on an elevated bed, off to the side of the room. The main light cast out from an immense white lotus. The flower drifted on his mist, its lily pad blanketing him. Lena went to her normal spot beside Selene and reached for his visible hand. It was soft but solid. He felt tangible.

As if on cue he called for her. "Lena."

"Hey. I'm here." She squeezed her grip. "I'm right here."

"Lena." His breath was short. "Kohl." He was gasping. "Lena."

Lena continued to stroke his hand. "No Kohl. Only me."

"Lena...." With this last name, Selene's voice drifted off.

Lena took a moment with him then turned towards Professor Nakshatra.

"Thank you, Lena. I know this seems small, but every little bit helps, especially at these end stages."

"I'll be back as soon as I can. He was asking for our friend Kohl too. Have you been able to connect with him?"

"Honestly this is the first time I've heard that name, but I'll look into it. I'll do whatever I can to set Selene up for success. He's come a long way from when I first saw him."

Lena couldn't deny that.

Her phone started chiming incessantly. She checked it warily. Twenty-two messages. "I have to go."

Professor Nakshatra's phone sounded too. "I guess we're both being summoned to Ward B, Miss Basil. I apologize in advance for what that must mean for your friend."

Dread spread throughout Lena's body. She finished her run without any distractions this time. She rushed straight to Airess. The healer's body lay limp, colorless. It was strange to see Airess so dull. Solei wept in the corner. Tao came up behind Lena and placed his hand on her shoulder.

"Sorry I took so long. I haven't caught up on everything." Lena shook her phone.

"It wouldn't matter if you did."

"You sound pretty down, even for you."

Tao sighed. "I don't know how we come back from this."

"Who is 'we'?"

"All of us. It's only a matter of time now."

"Tao, I'm sorry, but I've had a long day. Can you please be less ominous?"

"Look at her, Lena, she's already so different. She's changed."

"She's sick, Tao. People look different when they're sick."

Tao shook his head. "Look at her, Lena. I mean really look at her."

Lena focused hard but couldn't see another layer. There wasn't any special aura surrounding Airess' body. No fuzzy border. Airess was a normal body in a bed. *OMG. Airess was a normal body in a bed!*

"I saw this coming, but I prayed I was wrong."

Lena looked at Tao with her mouth still wide. "She's normal, Tao. She's absolutely normal." Tears were welling.

"I know. I've seen it too. Airess has lost all of her gifts. She's completely human now."

Chapter 13

Forgiveness and Faith

There was a lot of commotion around Airess' bed. Tao and Lena had been the first to notice the proud healer's transformation. The realization sparked a small panic among the staff at Ward B. Professor Nakshatra was in deep conversation with Nurse Galen; Lena overheard them trying to reach P.C. Solei sat even closer to Airess' bedside, shedding tears on the mossy blanket. Lena's heart broke for her friends. She hoped whatever was in Airess' mind now was happier than what her reality would be when she awoke.

Needing a break, Lena glanced around Ward B. It had only been a few weeks since her last visit, but things were already different. Kohl was gone now. That mermaid, or siren girl, what was her name? Lena couldn't remember, but she was gone now too.

Lena leaned back to stare at the hidden Ward A entrance on the far side of the hall. She gazed back to Airess. That might've been the start to all of the fights. Airess was always so protective of the things she cared about. Countless times Lena had found herself arguing over hypothetical situations only to be told she was overstepping into matters she didn't belong in. The trouble was, most of the time, Lena didn't even know what she was overstepping into. Though, admittedly, sometimes she did.

"Tao."

"Yeah, Lena?"

"I want to ask you something. I know it'll make you upset, but ... I still want to." Lena avoided eye contact.

Tao shifted in his seat, focusing more on Lena. He let the pause linger. "You want to know how much I knew about all of this?"

Lena's cringe gave her away.

"I don't know, Lena. Somewhere between too much and not enough. What I see, it's almost never enough, especially when I want to intervene; when I want to save someone I love." He was fidgeting. Inadvertently, Tao kicked the leg of Airess' bed.

Love. Lena decided to come back to that later. "Before the portal, you said you didn't want to be overly involved. What did you mean?"

"I meant I knew things were bad between everyone and they were only going to get worse. I didn't want to get caught up in it emotionally. I wanted to keep a clear mind to help as much as I could. I knew I could've told the team more information about Indra, but I wasn't sure if any of you would even want to know. I knew the faces entering and leaving Swarga would change, just like you'd see how Indra's would." Tears were starting to interrupt Tao's voice. "I knew the magical items were almost useless, but I could never bring myself to say that. And...." He took a deep swallow. "I knew." He wiped away his tears. "I knew one person in the group wasn't going to make it."

Tao took a moment to collect himself then turned back to Lena. "You have to believe me, though, that I never thought it'd be her." He quickly added, "Or you, or Solei." He waited for Lena to accept his plea before he continued. "I'd never let any of you walk into an outcome like that without saying or doing anything. I couldn't live with myself if I knowingly let you all get hurt. I'm struggling enough with how things are now."

Lena hugged him tight. "None of this is your fault, Tao. It's just what happens when humans get involved with gods. At least that's what my dad would say. Don't give up hope for Airess yet though. Who knows what happened to Professor Vontari and then Selene.... Well, hopefully Professor Nakshatra knows what she's doing." Lena checked the time. "And actually, I think I may have to check in with her. It's almost midnight." She scanned the area for the professor, no luck.

"Airess would want you to go. We all do, but I think I'm going to stay here if that's okay. I know I said I'd be there, but—"

"Stay. I'll be back as soon as I can." Lena gave him another squeeze then packed up.

Her first stop was Nurse Galen. She was mixing a balm made of lotus, the colors swirled playfully. After so many hours with Selene, that scent was a permanent fixture in Lena's brain. "Miss Galen, have you seen Professor Nakshatra?"

"Oh yes! She left only a minute ago; she said she had some final preparations to run before the big night. I bet you're pretty excited!"

Lena blushed. "Thank you."

"No problem at all! Please say hello to him, from me."

Lena used the secret passage and was soon back in the Ward A lobby. She was ready to get her Selene back. Butterflies and excitement filled her stomach. She signed in and was practically bouncing with joy. She had only taken a few steps when she ran into a very wet stranger and fell to the floor.

"Oh no! Lena! Are you alright?"

Lena noticed iridescently scaled legs while standing back up.

It was mermaid girl. Lena really needed to remember her name.

"Oh, hey. What are you doing here?" Lena shook off some strange algae from her hands.

The damp girl smelled of saltwater and fish. "I snuck in. I was trying to find you, kinda. All that magic got the best of me though, I felt queasy. I needed to find some water stat!" The girl made an awkward face. "But here we are now! I'm fresh from a saline fountain and you're right here next to me!"

"I'm sorry, but I can't stay. I have somewhere else I urgently need to be." *And now I get to be there smelling like a swamp creature.*

"Yes! Selene is his new name, right? Me too! That's why I'm here!"

Umm, what?

The former mermaid continued. "I knew if I could find you, I could find him. This is so great! Where do we go next?"

We? We do not go anywhere. This was not the new beginning with Selene that Lena had spent days imagining.

"Which way, Lena?" the mermaid prodded.

Not wanting to delay her arrival any further, Lena reluctantly guided the way.

~~~~~~~~~~~~~~~~~~~~~~~~~~~~~

Tranquility encompassed the room. The walls emulated the midnight hour to perfection. Stars twinkled brightly in the ceiling sky. Professor Nakshatra's lotus was plump and prominent as ever; they were already hard at work and in deep concentration. Her movements were mesmerizing. Lena couldn't help but feel her own body swayed by the motions of the professor's performance. The sweet scent of the white lotus filled Lena's senses and replenished her hopeful mood. She took her spot next to Selene.

She heard a crash behind her. She whirled around abruptly. Professor Nakshatra's concentration momentarily slipped, causing even more panic within Lena. Who knew what would happen if the ritual was interrupted.

The fishy girl waved to the professor. "Hi! I'm Delphine."

Lena was furious. *Can't you see she's busy? Why can't you just go away?*

Delphine, realizing that her introduction may have been ill-timed, knelt between Lena and the professor. This time, she whispered. "I'm his friend too. We met a few moments before The Bad One came. Still, it was easy to tell he was good, even if he was dressed ridiculously." No one responded. "My last memory of home was with Selene. He was trying to save me from The Death Bringer. He hadn't seen I'd already gotten hit. He freaked out when he saw." She chortled. Then, mocking Selene's voice, Delphine added, "You'll be okay. I'll take you to my home. We have healers there." She paused to give Lena a big smile. "Before he left this last time, he told me to find you if things went south. So, here I am! I did it!"

So you did, indeed. Lena was having a hard time keeping her attention undivided from Selene.

"Lena, it's time." Professor Nakshatra closed her eyes. Identical forms of the professor multiplied around them. Each version had a slightly different hue than the last— blues, greens, yellows, whites, and a singular red form. Several small lotuses of matching hues formed around the large, centered moonlike lotus. The colors contrasted starkly against the dark night air. Selene had begun to moan again. The figure Lena believed to be the original professor put her hands on the sides of his face and started chanting softly.

Somewhere, a gong of a clock sounded; a powerful gust of wind pushed through the room and then all went still. When Lena opened her eyes, all she could see was Selene. His body no longer looked like a flickering hologram engulfed in shadows. He looked real again; he felt real again. She threw herself over him in a hug and cried happy tears onto his chest. Feeling his chest rise and fall with his breaths was the best feeling Lena had felt in a long time. His hands shakily rose to her waist. Her grip on him tightened. He was finally home again.

"Hey. I know you all are having a moment, but should I do something for her?" Delphine's voice sounded uncertain.

Lena raised her head. Professor Nakshatra, whose skin was now a spring-green, lay upon an oversized leaf in the back of the room. Sighing, Lena gave Selene another hug and went to check on the professor. She appeared peacefully asleep.

"I think she's okay, but it's probably best to let the front desk know anyway."

Delphine remained stationary.

"Technically, I'm an apprentice here, so I suppose I should handle that." Lena scanned the room for some type of communication device. For a split second, she contemplated asking Airess for help before her memory caught up. "I'll have to walk back to the lobby."

Selene started coughing. Lena jumped over Delphine to get back to him.

"Hey. Hey. Shh. I'm here. Relax, everything's okay." She rubbed his hand in hers.

Selene barely opened his eyes. "Lena?"

"Yup. You're still stuck with me." She booped his now solid nose. "I've barely left."

Smiling proved to be easier for him than opening his eyes. He reached for Lena's face.

She leaned into his palm and draped her hands over his. "Everything's going to be okay."

Selene's tension eased. "Kohl?"

"No, no Kohl. He's not here. Maybe tomorrow."

Delphine tapped Lena's shoulder. "I think he means to ask if someone has taken care of Kohl."

Selene was getting antsy. "Kohl."

Lena was trying to hold him

steady while listening to whatever it was Delphine was trying to convey. "Why would someone need to take care of Kohl? Whatever you're saying is upsetting him. I think you should go."

Delphine laid her hand down on Selene's shoulder. "He asked me to keep an eye on Kohl while he went into the portal. I tried, but life here is a lot different than life at home. Things ended up being too difficult to manage. I couldn't do it and Kohl got away." Delphine's face had droplets falling from it. Lena wasn't sure if she was crying or just water-logged again.

Evaluating Delphine's message skeptically, Lena shifted closer to Selene. "Is Delphine right? Did you ask her to watch Kohl while you went into the portal?"

He nodded. "Kohl."

"Okay, you obviously need to rest more. Let me get you situated; then I'll go to the desk to ask about Professor Nakshatra, and I'll help Delphine look for Kohl. Deal?" Lena went to tuck him in.

Delphine grabbed Lena's arm. "Are you sure that's the best plan?"

Whilst removing Delphine's moist hand, Lena's voice did not conceal her snark. "Obviously, I do. Clearly, you disagree?"

Delphine could tell Lena was becoming irate. "Please don't be mad. I already failed your boyfriend once. I just don't want to let him down again. He drove The Death Bringer out of my home; I couldn't even keep tabs on him for a day. What if Selene is left alone and The Bad One comes here?"

Boyfriend? Lena's heart was leaping at that phrase. "We're not—"

"Please Lena. Can I stay with Selene? If the professor wakes up I'll go, I don't want to be somewhere I'm not welcome. It's just that, after everything he's done, I'd hate to fail him again."

"We don't have a death bringer here, Delphine."

Delphine was visibly confused. "What do you mean? We've all been in the same room together."

"I've been in the same room as The Death Bringer?" Lena was beginning to question how lucid Delphine's mind was.

"Yeah, Kohl was in Ward B with me when you were helping contain that supernova friend of yours." Delphine grimaced at the memory of Solei.

"Kohl's The Death Bringer? What does that even mean?" Lena felt like she just got punched in the gut.

"Yeah, you didn't know? It means he eliminates the godliness inside of someone. I agree that the name's dramatic, but he named himself. I think he likes the attention. But really, I thought everyone knew about him. His scent isn't subtle; he reeks of death. That was never off-putting to you?"

Lena stammered, unsure how to answer.

"I didn't expect you not to know. I thought you and Selene were, like, super close. Selene's been chasing Kohl for months. I assumed you both were. That's why I had to find you."

Lena glanced back at a twitching Selene. *Boy, what are you hiding with all your secrets?*

"Selene?" he called out. Evidently, he was still listening in on the girls' conversation.

"Yeah! Lena named you! Isn't it cute? I personally love it. It's the name of the moon goddess from my religion!" Delphine was overly excited to share that information.

Lena's mouth was wide open, but when Selene snuggled into her, she was able to let out a sigh of relief. He spoke his new name softly into her shirt as he drifted to sleep.

"So, when we all thought Kohl lost his powers, was that real or fake?" Lena was having a hard time processing all this.

"That was all part of the plan. Kohl needed toxins from whatever that water beast was. The speculation I heard was that he was trying to convert that fluid to be his blood. Selene tried to stop Kohl, but ... there were distractions." Delphine cut her sentence short.

"He got too distracted trying to save me." Lena finished for her.

"Your words, not mine."

"Fine. You stay here. Lock this door behind me; barricade it if you need to. I'll figure out what to tell the front desk, but this is a building filled with gods so they should be able to get past a stuck door if need be."

Delphine happily obliged.

Lena readied her things to go. "Do not leave his side, Delphine. It's the only option I hate more than leaving you alone with him."

~~~~~~~~~~~~~~~~~~~~~~~~~~~~

Lena had so much on her mind she was worried about letting something slip. She had to get a health check on Professor Nakshatra, some type of alert out about Kohl, and she'd promised a check-in on Airess. Touching base with Solei or Tao might be beneficial at this point too, but who knew what state they'd be in. Lena didn't want to put any more of a burden on them than what they were already facing. She made it to the front desk of Ward A in record time.

The lobby was oddly quiet. Lena rang the bell. No one came. "Hello?" she yelled. The normally bustling space was a ghost town. Lena peeked into the offices to attempt to spot movement but ultimately decided Ward B was her next best solution. Not knowing exactly how the magical front doors worked, she pictured Ward B as she passed through them and hoped for the best.

Elated at her success, Lena searched for Nurse Galen. She was only a few steps away. Ignoring whatever might have been going on there, Lena pulled the nurse over to her. At breakneck speed, Lena conveyed all the information she knew at once. By the end she wasn't sure if she was screaming her words or bawling them. Her face was red and covered with either tears or sweat. She felt beyond exhausted.

"Why don't you take a seat here and have a sip to drink, pet? I'll call Principal Chromwell and we'll try to sort this all out."

Lena did as instructed. "What is this? A medical aid?"

"It's a juice box. Apple juice, to be exact. Now, on to Professor Nakshatra. You said you thought she was asleep and green, is that right?"

Lena sipped her sweet drink and nodded.

"Okie dokie. We'll start there first then. You stay put." Nurse Galen muttered something to a nearby attendant, gave Lena a look, and disappeared behind a staff door.

Tao and Solei opened a side curtain. Lena waved them over. "How's Airess?"

"About the same," Solei said, pulling up chairs for themself and Tao.

"Sounds like things with Selene weren't as romantic as planned?" Tao goaded.

"Ugh. I know Delphine means well, but I wish she'd go away."

Lena's friends chuckled at her dismay. Solei nudged her. "Lena, I've seen how Selene is with you, both from my perspective and yours. He may be holding on to some secrets, but there's no way he protects anyone other than you that fiercely, including himself."

What Solei said helped. Lena had needed extra validation. "I know. It's just hard."

"I think that applies to everyone here and then some." Tao let out a big sigh. Lena wondered if he counted Kohl in that too. He had known him better than she had.

"Yeah? How are you holding up so far?" Lena offered some of her juice box.

Tao declined. "Not great, but at the same time obviously better than others. I know I shouldn't complain."

"Emotions aren't pie, Tao. Whatever you're feeling, big or small, that doesn't affect the size of someone else's feelings in the same situation. You don't have to lie about being great just because Airess has a bumpy road ahead of her," Lena said supportively.

"Especially in front of us," Solei added.

Lena emphasized, "Especially in front of us." She wanted to bring up Kohl but didn't know how. She wondered if the others had heard her earlier; that would make it a lot easier than repeating such hard words to say.

Tao was silent for a while and then whispered, "Hey. You know what?" He had the others' attention. "Emotions may not be like pie, but stressed spelled backwards IS desserts. I say, when everyone's able, we all go out for desserts to reverse our stress."

"You had me at 'dessert,' Tao Vovi." Solei smiled.

"Yum! Me too!" Lena replied, slurping the last of her drink.

Solei put their finger up to their lips and mouthed, "Nurse Galen's coming."

Lena tried to spot her visitor while her friends slid back over to Airess.

"Well, Ms. Basil, turns out not everything you said was complete gobbledygook. It took a minute, but I was able to track down Ipy at Ward A. She's checking on Professor Nakshatra as we speak. Principal Chromwell is aware of our request to see her, but I imagine that'll take time too. She has her hands full at the moment. Now, as for all that hogwash about poor Kohl, you should be gentler on that young man. He isn't a death bringer; he's just had a bad hand dealt to him in life. He's working through it." Nurse Galen bent down to Lena's eye level. "It'll get better, pet. Give it time." She held the moment until Lena seemed to accept her words. "Now—" The logo of Legacy Academy on Nurse Galen's badge started to blink in an ombré of colors.

I knew they had a way of communication! Lena attempted to eavesdrop.

Nurse Galen gave a hard press to the symbol and answered. "Yes, this is Nadea. Oh! Fantastic! Yes, she's still here, I'll let her know. Thank you so much for your help, Ipy. I can't imagine how busy you all are with your newest attendant. I appreciate you. Ha! Yes, you too now. Good night."

Lena couldn't hear anything on the other side. She was sure it was magically protected. She smiled brightly at the nurse, trying to invite further conversation.

"Don't strain yourself. All is well. Professor Nakshatra is indeed asleep. For that matter, Selene seems to be resting peacefully as well. Ipy has been kind enough to seal that room so, for the time being, occupants may leave freely but none may enter. And...." Nurse Galen was intentionally dangling a carrot. Lena was literally on the edge of her seat. The nurse tilted forward and whispered, "The previous guard has been relieved of their duties and sent back to her dormitory." Nadea winked.

Lena was ecstatic. Selene was safe, the professor was safe, and Delphine was gone. Sweeter words could not have been sung. "Do you mind if I ask one last question before I go?"

"Oh, I'm sure my preferences have little to do with what you kids tend to ask. Go ahead."

"Who's the newest resident in Ward A? It sounded like a big deal."

"You are quite tenacious, Miss Basil, but alas, that is not my information to give. I imagine Principal Chromwell will address you on those matters as she sees fit. Have a good night now."

"Yes ma'am, you too." Lena recognized that she was being dismissed. She crossed to the other side of the curtain to sit with her friends.

"Bold move, little cub. That's something usually only Tao would do." Solei sounded in better spirits.

Lena shrugged. "I wanted to know if it would give me any more information on Kohl." She spoke his name softly. Neither of her friends wanted to respond.

Tao went first. "Delphine's right."

Solei just about fell off Airess' bed. "Excuse me? What?"

He went on to explain. "I didn't know it was Kohl, but what she said is right. There's been a problem with the portals recently. Gods will enter Ward A, but sometimes there are stragglers that enter behind them. They're visibly not human, but they also don't seem to possess magic anymore either. Principal Chromwell has been unnerved about this for months. I've tried to help, but my visions never give enough information. Honestly, I thought it was Diablo for a long time. The sickness of the stragglers felt like something a devil's descendant could do; I thought it similar to Lucifer's fall from grace.

Plus, Diablo was almost always where the action was. That was about the only thing my visions helped with."

"You didn't blame him solely because his lineage traced back to Lucifer?" To everyone's shock, that question came from Solei.

"No. Of course not. I'd like to believe Airess didn't either. She was so close to Kohl and has always been naturally overprotective. The lines for her got blurry near the end, but I want to believe that the people I'm closest to can see past all the myths that are out there. I'd hope my inner circle is able to form their opinions of others based on their own experiences."

Lena went to speak, but Tao held her off. "Particularly, because this time I did not. I don't know if I can right my wrongs, but I have a wordy apology I'm prepared to give Selene the next time I have a chance."

"I didn't know people felt that way." Solei's voice was low but steady. "It's late. I need to go."

Lena and Tao exchanged confused looks.

"See you tomorrow, I guess?" Lena posed to Tao.

"Yeah, Lena. See you tomorrow." He rushed in the opposite direction of the exit.

Chapter 14
Lore and Love

Lena couldn't sleep. Her heart was restless. She craved to be back in Ward A. She wanted to help; she needed more information on Kohl. Deciding to head out early, she made breakfast for her parents and let them know where she was headed.

Finding Tao was first on Lena's list. He and Solei had acted strangely the previous night and Lena wanted to sort things out. She checked his favorite place to start—

the school library. Lena knew she wasn't supposed to be inside Legacy Academy but hoped that wasn't common knowledge. Much to her surprise, school was back in session. She tried to hide within the crowds. Classes would start in an hour and going around unnoticed would become harder then. She knew she had to work fast. When she reached her destination, it was desolate. Tao really did have one-of-a-kind interests. She wondered if he'd be back to his classes that morning, though it seemed unlikely. Lacking any other leads, Lena figured it was worth a shot.

She recalled the small corridors by her locker that Tao had shown her. She was tracing the crimson wallpaper with her finger when she began to hear a voice rise up. It belonged to Principal Chromwell.

"Yes Mr. Vovi, I too have a mastery of the occupants within my care. Some may even say it is better than yours."

"Principal Chromwell, I didn't mean—"

"Ah, and now, we have company. Please, before you make any other grand accusations against your fellow classmates, I advise that you and Miss Basil accompany me to Miss Hikona's bedside. I do believe Nurse Galen has hit a snag and is in need of assistance. Who better to aid her than two of my most illustrious students, yes? Come along now."

Tao and P.C. swept Lena up as they went. Principal Chromwell kept a brisk pace and enough space between her students to deter communication. The patients of Ward B were still waking up when the trio arrived. Airess' slumber endured the morning onset with Solei already by her side.

"Theodora! Thank you so much for coming so quickly. Students, you as well." Nurse Galen was not her usual composed self. "We're unfortunately facing a roadblock with our young friends' initial care here. Professor Nakshatra had intended to help Airess this morning; alas, it's been reported to me that she remains in and out of her dormant state. My staff has cultivated the necessary ingredients, I've memorized the incantation, but we lack the energy source of a star, which is unfortunately a dire need for Miss Hikona."

"A star?" Tao asked.

"I suppose, if you wanted to be incredibly specific, we are in need of a sun, but beggars can't be choosers. We agreed that a star should be a sufficient enough energy source before her transport begins."

"Airess is being transported?" Lena hadn't heard this mentioned before.

"Don't fret, Miss Basil, she'll be back. We're confident that a dip in god-bestowed waters is all she needs to finish her treatment," Principal Chromwell explained.

God-bestowed waters? What does that mean? That phrasing was foreign to Lena.

"They're more frequently called natural hot springs. The transportation is the easiest part." Tao spoke discreetly to Lena, easing her tension.

Solei remained focused on their friend. "I'll do it." The group was rightfully confused about their offer. "My surname, before I forewent it, was Morningstar." Solei stared directly at Tao and Lena as they spoke. "My family claims to have ties to the Goddess Aurora. She's essentially the personification of dawn in Roman culture. However, Lucifer tends to attract most of the attention in that bloodline. Depending on how you look at it, I am either the descendant of the light bringer or the descendant of the devil. I've never known what side of that line I'd fall on, but if Airess needs a star, then it'd be an honor to light her way home."

Lena didn't know what to say. Nurse Galen crouched next to Solei. "That's very brave of you, pet, but Airess needs more than a dazzling star, I fear. She needs to absorb a great deal of energy in order to regrow her powers, similar to the relationship between plants and the sun." Nurse Galen waited for Solei to show concern. They didn't. "I can't promise doing this will leave you unscathed."

Solei blew off the nurse's warning. "Nothing comes without its cost—lacrosse, the mist, the portal, being an heir of Lucifer. There's always some type of penance to pay."

Lena interrupted. "I've heard that combining powers can make them stronger. I don't know if the powers have to be similar, but I'd stand beside you in anything, Solei." She reached for her friend's hand.

Tao stepped over too. "Absolutely. If I can help, then I'm all in."

A tear fell from Solei's eye. "I was always scared to tell you, but especially after everything blew up about Diablo." They gave Lena's hand a squeeze.

"For the record, had you felt comfortable enough telling me, I'd have believed in you just the same," Lena said earnestly.

"Solei." Tao looked racked with guilt. "I won't deny that my poor track record precedes me. Nevertheless, since I've had the pleasure of knowing you, and I truly do mean that it has been a pleasure to know you, I'd want to believe that I'd support you regardless. I'm really sorry that even with your closest friends you felt the need to hold that in. That's on us, Solei, not you."

"Did you know?" Solei asked Tao. "I've always wondered."

"You all give me too much credit. I am as smart as I am clueless." He chuckled, lightening the mood.

"Solei?" It was Principal Chromwell.

"Yes ma'am?"

"If you remain willing, the time is nigh. Nurse Galen has finished her preparations."

"Tao and I want to help too." Lena spoke with authority.

Principal Chromwell's gaze shifted briefly. Her eyes appeared cloudy, almost milky white. Her free hand seamlessly waved over the eye of her staff. "All right, children.

I'll allow it. I shall caution you all, though, that letting another feel your essence is not something they are likely to forget. That type of connection should not be taken lightly."

· The decision was without debate and unanimous. Solei and Lena had already crossed that bridge twice and Tao was ready to finally offer something of value to his friends. A staff member closed the curtain surrounding Airess' bed, muting the outside noise. A sense of running water flashed over the group, only to be met by a breeze of fresh air filling their lungs. The background of Ward B faded away. Nurse Galen and Principal Chromwell flanked the former healer symmetrically above her head. The triad of friends centered around Airess' feet. Silently, Solei was instructed to streamline their energy into a misshapen globe hovering slightly atop the group. The three followed suit and closed their eyes.

Solei harnessed and released their radiant prowess onto the item. Tao channeled his ambition and determination. His devotion to those around him metamorphosed into energy surging from his palms to his target. Lena concentrated, not on her specific skills but the source within her that Gabriel evoked when she fell into the rings. The scintillating brilliance she felt burning within her core. The light she had often tried to ignore, and suppress subconsciously, in order to fit in. The fire she had now grown to love and nurture. It was the quality Lena cherished most about herself. She isolated her energy flow in her mind and unleashed her power onto the swelling sphere.

Once the dimension of a small marble, the globe had enlarged to an unforeseen size. Only a portion of the circumference remained visible. The orb was molten. Lena opened her eyes to watch waves of lava swirl on the structure's surface. Nurse Galen was deep in prayer. She spoke in elegant Japanese prose. When her voice subsided, Principal Chromwell waved a wooden plaque before the nurse.

Nadea bowed slightly, in thanks, and held it to her chest until its blank face was imprinted with feelings only her heart could convey. Once complete, Nurse Galen elevated it boldly above her head, arms outstretched, until it was absorbed by their surroundings. Panels traveled in front of the other party members as well, where they promptly replicated the nurse's demonstration. Designs and drawings filled the backdrop. Their entire space was covered in a rotation of well wishes and love. Then their world slowed to a stop. The serene environment pulled away leisurely and, in time, the group found themselves back behind a curtain at Ward B. When the sounds, smells, and sights returned to normal, Airess let out a cough. She smiled towards her three friends.

A staff member pulled back the privacy curtain to assist Nurse Galen in checking Airess' vitals. Lena noticed a minty-green Professor Nakshatra waiting to greet the crew and with her was Selene in a wheelchair. Lena waved over to the boy, who smiled and waved back.

"I'm impressed. I told Selene we needed to make haste because I was sure my talents were imperative to the situation, but things appear to have gone flawlessly. Congratulations Nadea. As always, your capabilities are astonishing," Professor Nakshatra commented humbly.

"Thank you, Tara, but this credit is not mine to receive. It belongs to our young bringer of dawn right here and their friends. The strength of these three hearts is far more capable than what my old hands can cobble together. I'm immensely proud of the four of you." She lightly stroked Airess' hair. "I want to perform a full examination on Airess and share a minute with her. Also, today's trinity of heroes need to be checked over as well."

"Fantastic! You all are so exemplary! While our brave young scholars tend to their medical needs, I wonder if I may have a word with you please, Professor?

Alone, perhaps?" Principal Chromwell asked Professor Nakshatra.

Lena went with her friends, grabbing Selene's wheelchair along the way. Solei lay down on the examination table while Tao sat in a chair close by. Lena was about to grab another chair when Selene accidently tripped her. He caught her as she stumbled and pulled her into his lap.

"Oops," he said with a big grin. She blushed, rolling her eyes at him, and settled into his arms. He whispered into the crook of her neck, "Nothing compares to you, but it's incredible to see Solei's mind at peace. Their duality tore them apart constantly."

"You knew?" Lena's pitch rose in surprise. It caught the attention of Tao. Selene laughed off her expression.

"Are you guys talking about Kohl?" Tao inquired.

"Oh my gosh! I almost forgot! How could you not tell me about that?!" Lena playfully smacked Selene's chest.

"There was no way I was going to be able to convince Airess of what I knew and I wasn't going to make things worse between the two of you. Plus, you were going through a lot and not always handling it well...." He braced himself for another thwack, but Lena was too busy glaring at him. "Not to mention, I obviously had my own trust issues and secrets to bear. I wasn't ready to let other people in yet."

"And now?" Solei turned to their side, facing Selene.

"And now ... now I'm working on it. I'm giving it my best shot."

Selene's words resonated with Tao. "Me too, brother. Me too." Tao let their thoughts linger. "Actually, I wanted to share something. Last night, after talking with Solei and Lena, I went to the library. There was something in our conversation about devils and the dead that struck me. It brought back vague memories of some Slavic texts I read once. Naturally, I scoured all the books I could pull to try to find what I was looking for. It took a while, but I finally got it. Selene, am I right in thinking that Kohl is considered a living vampire?"

"I've never heard that term before, but I know he speaks of having two souls. His biggest problem is when he leaves his body, especially during sleep. That's how I got mixed up with him. I spend a good portion of my time in the realm of dreams." He bumped Lena with a smirk. "When Kohl leaves his body, he isn't himself. I've seen his other side do some pretty awful things. The kid has a good mind to him when he's able, but he has some real serious issues he faces daily. He wanted the toxin of the serpent to merge his two sides. He thought the poison would subdue his god-given side and keep him conscious more frequently. He is so desperate to control himself that he enters, or creates, horrible situations. Before the portal, Kohl was becoming increasingly paranoid that his other side was taking over. He hates his powers so much, but I've always felt that his hate only fuels The Death Bringer more. I could never get him to listen. That's what he calls it by the way, The Death Bringer, or The Bad One. All The Death Bringer wants is chaos and anarchy. That side of him is set on destroying everything it can with a fury."

"I can't even imagine carrying all that by your lonesome," Lena said empathetically.

"I don't know what to do, and now he's completely off my radar. Either side of him could be anywhere."

"You don't have any leads?" Solei asked gently.

"Portals? Maybe? That's where he hid the magical items he stole from the field." Selene reflected on some of Kohl's recent actions. "Going into the homes of the gods, and taking away what makes them special, is a favorite pastime of his," he added grimly.

"He's why Legacy keeps getting so many additional entrants after a god comes to Ward A," Tao connected.

"Yeah, they're all like Delphine—conspicuously unhuman

but also unable to retain magic. It's the worst of both sides. They're not meant for our world and literally would not be able to survive going back to theirs." Selene's volume was escalating. "It's cruel and heartless. I've made myself sick over this for months."

"Students." Principal Chromwell had joined them. "It seems I have some apologies that have come due." Professor Nakshatra and Nurse Galen accompanied her. Airess was even able to tag along in her own wheelchair. "I listened in on part of your exchange. We all did, actually. Fortuitously, our most recent rescue shared similar thoughts upon waking. Airess has reiterated claims

Mr. Vovi provided to me earlier. My pride seems to have obstructed my judgment. I am now in agreement that we do indeed have a rather large complication to confront. In lieu of this recent revelation, I have asked Professor Nakshatra to lengthen her intended stay indefinitely. She has graciously agreed but on a stipulation that involves one of you. Professor Nakshatra, if you will." Principal Chromwell escorted Lena off to the side, letting the professor step forward.

Professor Nakshatra knelt down to be at eye level with Selene. "Young sir, I have watched you grow from mere particles to a fully functional being. In doing so,

I've acquired a great deal of knowledge. I've been reminded of the importance of patience and learned of the misfortunate tribulations you've had in your life. Your will inspires me. I would sincerely appreciate an opportunity to teach you how to harness the wonders of the moon more effectively. I feel compelled to divulge that our powers are not fully parallel. Despite that information, I do believe what I'm offering you is of great value. I would like you to consider this new path in your life's journey."

She just asked him to be her protégé! Lena was exceedingly happy for him and marginally jealous.

"Wow. No one has ever asked for my company before. I would be honored. Would I be able to stay here? I think, for the first time in my life, I may actually have friends. I'd hate to abandon that."

The group of four concurred. Professor Nakshatra bowed in consent. "It's official then. Theodora, I'd be honored to join you here at Legacy Academy."

"Marvelous! I—" The principal was cut off by her blinking badge. Nurse Galen's badge blinked too. Chromwell held up her hand as she excused them both.

Solei sat upright to address Airess. "How ya holding up? Good to see you back."

"So far so good. I really appreciate what you all did for me."

"You don't have to thank us, Airess," Tao interjected.

"No, I do. I haven't quite found the words I want to say yet. Nadea explained everything to me. We knew my talents only had so much time left; it's part of why I'm her apprentice. Knowing my healing was limited scared me. I wanted to be able to fix everything going on here before they ran out. I got kind of carried away, perhaps slightly overly patronizing too." With that, she maneuvered to face Lena. "I can't adequately say how sorry I am about the way I acted before the portal; how I acted towards Diablo specifically. I was tragically self-righteous."

"Things are different now. I think we can all recognize that?" Lena looked to Selene for confirmation.

"All we can do now is try our best, right?" Selene reiterated.

"I agree. Thank you all again. Truly." Airess' delivery was almost mousy.

"Did Kohl do this to you?" Solei probed.

"No. This is how I develop. My powers have a life cycle. Not unlike the plants I grow and the people I heal. It's all a part of who I am. I struggle to accept it though."

"Folks, I think we have a theme here." Tao impersonated an announcer. Everyone groaned at him, including the professor. The other adults were re-entering the scene.

"Ms. Hikona, it seems you had the finale of a century before your grand exit. A very important angel has opened their eyes and it appears they're asking for you," Principal Chromwell shared with pride.

Excitement buzzed all around. They hurried giddily to Ina's room. It was barely recognizable. The overgrown plants that once concealed it were gone. The atmosphere had shifted from greenhouse to glamorous. The space was ornamented with multicolored lights stemming from picturesque stained-glass windows hung up high. A decor of books, scrolls, and tapestries lined the walls. Staring in amazement, the group continued on until they found a small rotunda of forest-like paradise. Ina was sitting on a bench admiring a babbling brook that seemed to flow through the circular space. Robust trees encompassed the perimeter. Moss and plants outlined Ina's sitting area.

She gazed over to Airess. "I'm so glad you came! I've been eager to show my appreciation." Ina's form was fuzzy when she spoke. "I'm forever grateful for your kindness and care, Miss Hikona.

There were many dark years before you brought such vigor back into my life. I shall never be able to show my full gratitude, but know you always have a friend in me." The angel needed to take a breath. "I hope I'm still remembered as a desirable ally after all this time." Ina winked at former comrade Theodora.

"For the rest of our days," Principal Chromwell responded in kind.

"I hope you don't mind my redecorating. You created a lovely bounty of life around me while I slept, but this is slightly more my style," Ina shared happily.

"Of course not! Please lift the spells off your house too. I would normally offer, but I have yet to restart my casting's biorhythm. Once I'm rehabilitated, I would love to share some time with you. I'm in such awe seeing you now," Airess implored.

"Of course, of course. I apologize for not recognizing the change within you sooner. I am still getting my wits about me." Ina analyzed the group before her. "You know, deep in my slumber I swore I felt a touch of angel nearby." She scanned the crowd. "That must have been you. Have you visited me often as well?"

The question was directed at Lena. She was not prepared to answer it. "Umm, yeah, you know, sometimes." *Mostly when I had come to fight with Airess or needed to be smuggled somewhere.*

Ina had a silly grin about her. "I see then. You actually look quite familiar, but I can't imagine we've ever met."

"Her name is Magdalena Basil, Ina." Principal Chromwell waited for the last name to register. "She's Kasim and Kamilah's daughter. They recently relocated back to Astoria. In fact, your house happens to be where I first met Miss Basil. You're practically neighbors."

The Old Hag's house. Ina was the Old Hag. Those rumors couldn't have been less accurate.

"Kamilah?" Ina's tone was downcast; her form's solidity quivered.

"Principal Chromwell took her to see you not too long ago. I'm sure she'd love to see you again." Lena tried to sound reassuring, but Ina had begun to weep. Her tears became more tangible than her body.

Principal Chromwell and Nurse Galen rounded everyone up to leave when Ina pleaded one last request. "Please visit again soon." Even with so few words, her voice carried sorrow and hope. Lena would be sure to come back with her parents as soon as they accepted her invitation.

Principal Chromwell closed the door behind the group. "What an eventful day we've all been able to share together! Shall we all be going our own ways now?"

"I would like to take Airess back to Ward B to continue to monitor her health. She and I can start planning her departure tomorrow. That'll include finding an assistant to tag along with us." The quintet gathered for an immense group hug. Lena made sure Selene was added in too. Nurse Galen and Airess set off.

The rest of the members bid adieu to one another and headed towards their respective homes. Lena agreed to push Selene to his mainstay in Ward A.

"If you live here, why do you always sign in?" Lena asked as she walked.

"I must like the attention," Selene jested.

"You make no sense."

"Hey, this is it. Help me up?"

Lena locked the chair and assisted him. He opened his door to a familiar seaside cave.

"You," Lena said, still holding him steady.

"Me." Selene caressed the side of her face. "Do you remember how I promised if we made it out of the portal I'd tell you another pearl of wisdom?"

"I do." She savored his touch.

"It took me a while, but I think you walking me home safely constitutes us making it out of the portal. What do you think?"

Lena's cheeks grew hot. "Seems that way to me too."

Selene smoothly slipped his hand past Lena's cheek to the base of her neck. His other hand curved around her waist, pulling her closer. He paused for a moment. Lena draped both her arms loosely around his neck and nudged his nose with hers. Her heart was racing, her breaths were paralyzed. Selene leaned in cautiously, offering the softest of kisses upon her lips. Her lips ached for more. Giving into desires formed long ago, they held on to each other tightly and kissed deeply. The rest of the world dissolved around them.

Epilogue
Sunshine and Serendipity

Winter was in full swing, but the Basils were preparing for their first tropical vacation. Life had become exceptionally hectic in the months following Ina's restoration and they were all ready for a break.

"Mom! I can't find my flip-flops!"

"Magpie, I already packed those when I found them in the

freezer. Millie, sweetheart, do you know where my swim trunks are?"

"They're in the swimming pool! Our snorkel masks are there too!"

"We don't have a swimming pool, do we?" Kasim poked his head into Lena's bedroom.

"Ina does." Selene was the first to answer.

"Right! I'll text her. Also, off the bed, young sir. You know the rules."

Lena shot her boyfriend a glance that said, "I told you so."

Selene got off the bed and embraced Lena from behind, kissing her shoulder. "He didn't catch this, though, did he?"

"I did!" It was Kamilah.

"Hey Mom, you need help with something?" Lena offered, distracted.

"Yes! Please! I'm struggling to close up this darn suitcase!"

Lena went into the hallway to tend to the luggage her mom was dragging. "You can let go; I got it. You'd think Dad and Solei could've created an item to resolve this." While she knelt to pull the zipper, something sharp jabbed her palm. "Ouch!" Lena opened up the bag to examine its contents. There were pineapples inside. Dozens of pineapples. "Mom, do you think we really need so many?"

"Oh yes, my love! The pineapple is the symbol of warm welcomes, celebration, and hospitality! I saw that on the TV. I'd hate to go to a new country and have them think ill of us. My only regret is not being able to fit in more! Who knows how many people we will meet?"

Selene came over and zipped it up. "Don't go stealing all the credit now, Mrs. Basil. I'll help close your bag, but you gotta share when it comes time to hand them out. Deal?"

Kamilah beamed. "You can come with me during every presentation!"

"You got it. Also, I may have some room in my luggage downstairs. It's by the front door if you want to check."

"That would be perfect!" She ran to the floor below.

"I'll carry this one down for her; are you about done with yours, Lena? I think your bag is heavier than the load of pineapples," he teased.

"You enable her so much. I do not want to hear you complain that you have to walk around handing out pineapples to the locals while I'm lying on the beach enjoying myself."

Selene shrugged. "She's family. I can lie on the beach at home. If distributing fruit makes her happy, then I say let's go find more fruit."

"You're good to her. I think it's why my dad hasn't banished you from our house ... yet." Lena shuffled her suitcase out into the hall and handed it to Selene. She kissed him on the cheek as she passed him to go down the stairs.

"You're confident these waters are clear? I'm not sure I'm comfortable with you potentially swim-ming with sharks, Lena." Her dad was reading the printouts of their destination on the counter for the millionth time.

"Dad, you've heard Nurse Galen, Airess, and Delphine all rave about how amazing this place is. We're already packed. This is happening. It'll be okay, I promise."

"I am aware of their opinions. How did Delphine describe it? Amazeballs?" Kasim looked disturbed. "I even understand why it's important that we meet them there to check on the potential progression of Delphine's abilities, but I still feel the swimming pool of the school would have been a much more practical solution."

"That is not how these trials work and you know that. I know you do because you and Solei were the ones who told me."

"Have you heard from them lately?" Kasim's tone lowered.

"No. Not since they went back home for break. I wish they would've stayed at Legacy. If they didn't want to be alone, they could've come with us or stayed with Ina. Solei was just determined to go back to Rome."

"It's hard letting people we love chart their own course. I have felt that first-hand."

Lena hugged her dad tightly. "Thank you."

"Hey, Mr. Basil, we have four suitcases ready to go, but does Mrs. Basil have a bag packed with her belongings?"

Kasim groaned. "I forgot to do that. I'll be right back." He called into the backyard. "Millie, can you meet me upstairs, please?"

"Speaking of absent text messages, has Tao completed his deep meditation yet? He should be coming out of it soon, right?" Lena asked.

"Last I heard from P.C. was that he was still in his trance. She was hopeful he'd be ready with information any day now, but nothing yet. I hope it works. It's been months without being able to track down Kohl and The Nulls keep adding up. Professor Nakshatra and I harbored five more this week alone."

Lena sighed. "Yeah, I really hope we can figure out how to give them some of their essence back after this trip. There's a lot of pressure for these trials to go well. I hope Delphine is managing it all right."

"She has Airess and Nurse Galen close by. Those three have been inseparable since they went for Airess' rehabilitation. Plus, she's Delphine. There isn't a lot that fazes her."

Lena giggled. "That's true. Oh! Hey, look!" She tore off a page from her mom's daily calendar. "Guess what today is?"

Selene reached for her hands and kissed each one. "Is it our two-month anniversary?"

"You knew!" Lena's cheeks turned red as she smiled.

"Of course I knew. I'd never forget you."

"Me neither." Lena wrapped her arms around him and they held on to each other's embrace until Kasim came back.

"All right. I think that does it. We should be all set to go now. You kids ready?"

The couple was still holding hands. "Ready," they said in unison.

"Me too!" Kamilah added, wrapping her arm through Kasim's, her other was holding an additional pineapple.

"Okay, stay close. On the count of three. One. Two. Three!" Kasim threw a disc onto the ground, opening up a portal to their desired destination.

As it closed behind them, Selene's call echoed. "Anything but seaweed!"

Acknowledgments

First and foremost, I want to thank Nitish Mathpal. Without you, this book simply wouldn't have come into existence. You've spent hours helping me smoothen out the book's content and been a constant throughout this whole process. Not to mention, the book cover you have created is beyond anything I would've expected. I can't describe how grateful I am for all your time and your friendship. P.S. Thanks for not rage-quitting when we both realized my definition of what a question is is not the actual definition of what a question is.

I also want to thank my family—especially Brian and Annabelle. Writing and creating a book takes time, a lot of time. The patience and space you have given me are so incredibly appreciated and made this dream possible. Not only have you supported me in prioritizing this dream over other activities but also you have done the same and made sacrifices on end for me. I love you all to the moon and back.

Additionally, there are countless thanks I want to send out to others that are close to me. This has been a work in progress for many years now and I cannot count how many times I've reached out to various friends asking for their thoughts on one thing or the other—character arcs, mythology, design choices, wording—I've asked them all to so many of you. Thank you for always being supportive, for always giving me constructive feedback, and, most importantly, for always being there. You all have the kindest of hearts and I'm grateful for each and every one of you.

Last, but not least, thank you to our editor Ken for all their hard work and for completing such a tight turnaround.

About the Author

A. P. Goodman is a lifelong enthusiast of mythology and religion. From her first love of Disney's Hercules to her most recent love of Krishna, A. P. Goodman has spent much time engrossed in various accounts of past and present lore. She loves obscure stories best and feels strongly that no tale should be left untold.

In her moments outside of exploring cultural deep dives, nothing compares to warm Chai tea and sharing her time with loved ones. Her husband, daughter, best friends, brother, and fluffy puppy are always her favorite company. She also has two meddlesome cats. Legacy Academy is her debut novel.

www.ingramcontent.com/pod-product-compliance
Lightning Source LLC
Chambersburg PA
CBHW030741030726
47497CB00001B/88